"If I can't take the kids this time, it seems you'll do." The kidnapper's scratchy voice filled her right ear.

"I'm not leaving empty-handed," he continued, sending a chill down her spine.

The man squeezed her tighter around her torso. She struggled as he growled, "Now who's sorry she tried to play the hero? Huh?"

"Help," she yelled, praying someone would hear.

The back door burst open. James filled the doorway.

James yelled something she didn't register as the kidnapper snarled and let go of her.

His right hand reached into his jacket and pulled out a jagged knife.

Rachel gasped, paralyzed.

James stepped forward, and his foot whipped out a kick so fast that if Rachel had blinked she would've missed it. The knife soared into the hallway. He pinned the man down.

"Who sent you?" James asked.

Heather Woodhaven earned her pilot's license, rode a hot-air balloon over the safari lands of Kenya, parasailed over Caribbean seas, lived through an accidental detour onto a black-diamond ski trail in the Aspens and snorkeled among stingrays before becoming a mother of three and wife of one. She channels her love for adventure into writing characters who find themselves in extraordinary circumstances.

Books by Heather Woodhaven

Love Inspired Suspense

Calculated Risk
Surviving the Storm
Code of Silence
Countdown

COUNTDOWN

HEATHER WOODHAVEN

HARLEQUIN® LOVE INSPIRED® SUSPENSE

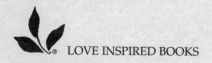

LOVE INSPIRED BOOKS

Recycling programs
for this product may
not exist in your area.

ISBN-13: 978-0-373-67778-8

Countdown

www.Harlequin.com

Printed in U.S.A.

God setteth the solitary in families.
–Psalms 68:6

To Jennifer Brost.
I love the way you and The Job Foundation
walk with children and their families. You are an inspiration
and a constant source of encouragement.

ONE

Rachel Cooper whipped the steering wheel to the left, maneuvered through the rush-hour traffic and entered her tree-lined subdivision. Her shoulders relaxed. Each time she made the turn it was as if she'd left the city behind.

Her stomach growled at the smell of the steak burrito and *chile con queso* sitting in the paper sack on the passenger seat. The night's agenda included lounging on the couch and watching her favorite shows. The idea seemed like the perfect remedy to the physical strain of styling hair for twelve hours. After a couple hours of loafing, she'd make herself burn away the calories with her nightly kickboxing video…if she didn't justify her way to an early bedtime instead.

Rachel guided the car around the maze of bends and curves within the subdivision. Not a single street lasted more than a couple of blocks before turning and changing names. The real-estate agent explained the layout was to prevent cars from speeding, but Rachel imagined it was more about fitting as many houses as possible on the amount of land.

Giant oak trees bordered her sky-blue house. To the rest of the neighborhood she owned the smallest house in the affluent subdivision, but to her, it represented the mark of how far she'd come in life. The other houses encircled the small home in the quiet cul-de-sac of the dead-end street.

Her neighbor, James McGuire, owned the house just past hers. His three-year old twin boys exited their garage on training-wheel bikes, racing each other down the driveway. Rachel pressed on the brake, even though she was still over a block away.

It had become habit to slow down at the sight of children. They rarely ever watched for cars within the subdivision, most likely due to the lack of traffic. In such a family-oriented place, everyone watched out for each other's kids. If Rachel were the type to want kids, the neighborhood would've been ideal.

A white van took off from its parked position opposite her house, turned one hundred and eighty degrees and screeched to a stop in front of the twins. Her stomach fluttered. Odd, but maybe the driver hadn't noticed the kids before.

The driver and a passenger jumped out of the van and ran for the boys. Each man grabbed a kid off the bikes. The boys kicked wildly, but their fight didn't slow the men down. They threw the boys through the side door of the van.

Rachel slammed on her brakes and stared, unsure of what to do. Her stomach twisted. Was she really witnessing a kidnapping?

One man bounded into the van right after the kids as the driver jumped in behind the wheel and took off. The van screeched and barreled toward her vehicle. *Lord, give me wisdom.*

The van would pass her in less than five seconds. Rachel pressed the call button on her steering wheel and hit the gas. She swung the car around, positioning it diagonally across the road in hopes she could block the van. They couldn't pick up enough speed this close to cause real damage, could they?

"Call 9-1-1." Her voice shook, but the ringing through the speakers bolstered her courage as she tensed every muscle in her body, preparing for impact.

The van honked loudly. Thoughts of the boys bouncing around in the cargo area of the van made her question the decision until she thought of kids on the news…kidnapped and gone forever.

She'd risk the boys getting banged up a little if it meant saving their lives. Though, if the men tried to drive through her blockade, she'd be the one in for a world of pain. Rachel tucked her chin to her chest, cringing. She focused on the ringing. *Come on. Answer the phone.*

She dared a peek out of her right eye. The van drew close enough that she could see through the approaching windshield, and for the briefest moment, the driver's glare met hers. He wasn't slowing down.

She pressed back into the seat, in the worst game of chicken she'd ever imagined. The van bounced up and over the curve and clipped the front of her car. Her spine jolted to the left. A searing pain rushed up into her neck. The impact spun her car in the opposite direction of her house as the van drove over a set of lavender bushes and smashed into a mailbox.

An airbag deployed from her passenger side, and a light powder misted over everything. She turned her head to the side, but nothing came out of her steering wheel, most likely because she hadn't been in motion when the van hit that side of the car.

The van pressed onward and back onto the street.

In the rearview mirror her neighbor—James—sprinted down the street, yelling. She couldn't let those boys be separated from their father. Coughing away the powder, Rachel stomped on the gas pedal.

"Nine-one-one. What is your emergency?"

"Two men kidnapped my neighbor's boys." Rachel rattled off the address as she pressed the gas pedal into the car's flooring. If they took that long to answer the phone, could she really trust they'd stop the kidnappers in time? If she managed to get close enough to see the license plate, though, the likelihood the police would catch them increased.

Her fingers squeezed around the steering wheel, and she pressed her left heel into the car door for balance as she made the hairpin turn. Her heart seemed stuck in her throat, and her stomach lurched.

The dispatcher said something, but the words sounded like mumbling. It took all her focus to drive through the subdivision at as high of a speed as the turns allowed. She believed the real-estate agent about short streets stopping speeders now. The van's left wheels lifted off the asphalt for the briefest of seconds on a sharp turn.

The voice coming through her speakers repeated something. Although Rachel's listening skills sometimes proved lacking when she was focused, her mouth never failed to operate. She could always talk while she worked. Knowing the streets in the neighborhood by heart, she shouted out the name of each one at each turn.

So far all the trees and the green front yards were empty of little feet. *Please keep the rest of the kids in the neighborhood inside, Lord.* Hopefully most of them were at their after-school activities or already at home eating dinner.

Rachel gritted her teeth on the only straight stretch before the subdivision ended. If the kidnappers reached Overland Drive, a main city road, they'd only need to go a few blocks before hitting the freeway.

If they succeeded, the van could easily hide in the traffic or take one of the many exits available to escape. The odds of bringing the boys back home would drop, and she couldn't bear to tell James, who had already lost his wife tragically, that his sons might not ever come home.

The whir of her engine grew louder at the increased speed. Ten feet away. She pressed her toe harder into the pedal. She pulled close enough only to see…nothing. No license plate. A weight dropped into her gut. "No, no, no."

She should've known.

Sirens wailed, growing louder. Rachel braced herself for the final turn out of the subdivision. The white van squealed to a halt, sliding sideways. She gasped as she flew at high speed toward it. She slammed her foot on the brake, her body thrown back into her seat. *Please don't let me hit the boys.*

She squeezed her eyes shut and forced the brake to the floor. A high-pitched squeal preceded a sudden stop. The momentum flung her torso toward the steering wheel. Searing pain rushed up through her ribs from the impact. She opened one eye and judged the remaining distance between her bumper and the white van—eight feet to spare. The car choked and died.

She exhaled.

A man with shaggy brown hair shot out of the passenger door and scowled at her. Her heart stopped as he ran toward her, his hands in fists. She slapped the lock button three times— just to be sure. The car locks clicked each time, as if attempting to reassure her.

The man slammed a fist into the hood and pulled out a gun from his jacket. She flinched. Her eyes flitted around the car for a possible weapon. She could throw the nacho dip in his face, but how much time would that buy? Why weren't the cops running around the van to help her?

The back of one cruiser and the top of another were barely visible due to the dip in the road at the front of the subdivision. More "speed control" at work. The driver still sat in the white van. The officers probably had their sights and, hopefully, their weapons, trained on him. So they were clueless about this guy on the loose.

The man walked around the front of her car. He stared at her with calculating eyes. He pointed the weapon at her and made a come-hither hand signal. Rachel gasped. He wasn't looking to exact revenge. He wanted to use her as a hostage. To get away or to get the boys again? Or both? She inhaled sharply. The dispatcher. "Are you still there?" Her voice squeaked.

No one responded. She turned the ignition. It released an awful grinding noise as if telling her it wouldn't take any more of her abuse today. With one hand, she flipped open the console between the seats and felt for the hard plastic handle of her emergency escape tool.

On one end, the pointed steel hammer ensured she'd be able to shatter the vehicle windows if needed. She imagined it'd pack a potent punch against an attacker, as well. She shoved it into her jacket pocket on the remote chance she was put in a hostage situation.

Lord, bring help. She forced a façade of bravery and returned the man's glare. The kidnapper seemed unfazed as he approached. She needed to get the police's attention before he succeeded, but how?

James McGuire slapped the steering wheel. He'd lost sight of the back of Rachel's maroon SUV. He couldn't see where they'd gone. "Don't take them away from me, too. I can't—" The words stuck in his throat. The unbidden memory of being told his wife had been killed rushed to the forefront of his mind.

He gritted his teeth and didn't let up as the Dodge Charger jumped over a curb. He took each curve at a diagonal. He jerked his gaze from north to south at each side street as he barreled toward the east exit of the subdivision.

Caleb and Ethan... His eyes stung from pent-up anguish and rage. A horn in the distance blared and didn't let up. He sped closer and closer to the exit. The horn grew louder. "Please," he groaned aloud. If ever he needed the Lord to hear his cry...

He shot past the final corner. The white van sat parked across the subdivision entrance. His mouth went dry at the sight. They'd been stopped? His boys...were they? The horn continued to blare, the noise coming from Rachel's SUV. Had she crashed? A man at her driver's door lifted a gun toward her window while his other hand gestured for her to get out. His car windows muffled shouted words from a police officer's megaphone. They wouldn't get to her in time. Had they already pulled his boys to safety?

The Charger revved and responded immediately the moment he shifted into high gear. James aimed the nose of the car for the man. The squeal of the tires finally got the man's attention, his eyes wide, but the gun remained trained on Rachel. The man's face contorted as if trying to make sense of where the car planned to go.

James squinted and blocked out the rest of his surroundings. He would not lose another woman in his life to senseless violence. For half a second he questioned whether he should spare the man that laid a hand on his children. His heart squeezed, his neck tingled, and James exhaled as he slammed on the brake. The car skidded to a stop a centimeter away from the man's legs.

The kidnapper jumped backward, as if trying to get out of the way, at the sound of squealing brakes. His face paled as if he was unsure James had actually stopped. The man's arms flailed. He fought for balance and lost. The gun slipped from his fingertips as he fell to the pavement.

James thrust the car into Park and jumped out. He stepped toward the kidnapper, prepared to fight him if necessary to keep the gun from his reach. The man had already jumped to a crouched position and glanced between the gun and James. Most likely he was trying to judge if he could make it to the weapon before James pounced.

James balled his hands into fists in response. The kidnapper snarled and sprinted past the nose of Rachel's car, disappearing behind the closest house.

The police fanned around the van, guns drawn, but pointed their weapons at the driver who had his hands up in the air. They didn't run after the other man. Had they not known there were two of them? James couldn't allow him to escape.

Police cars screeched to a stop behind them. One cruiser squeezed past Rachel's car and ramped up a driveway before two officers jumped out and pursued the kidnapper on the run. James relaxed his hands.

Rachel stepped onto the pavement. The slight breeze moved her glossy, thick hair away from her pale face and wide eyes. James ran to her and grabbed her shoulders, looking for signs of shock. "Are you okay?"

She trembled underneath his fingers but nodded rapidly. His gaze jerked back to the van swarmed with officers. He fought back the urge to run over and wrench the van door open, but he watched everyone on high alert. The last thing he wanted was to escalate the situation and to give them any reason to delay opening the door to his boys.

He pulled Rachel to his chest, his chin grazing the top of her head. Her body shook, and he held her tight. *Please let my boys be okay.*

An officer near the white van ran toward them. The cop spoke into his radio and waved his hand, indicating Rachel and James should stay back. Other officers pulled the driver out of the van. They pressed the man against the hood and proceeded to handcuff him.

Rachel pulled away from James but grabbed for his hand. Any other moment and he would've felt uncomfortable with her touch for reasons he'd take days to analyze. But now, at this moment, it was as if they stood together in prayer, in unity, during the most excruciating wait of his life.

The side door of the van slid open. Inside the cargo area, on the floor of the van, the twins clung to each other. His eyes burned, his throat tightened, and a wretched bark of relief escaped.

The boys were safe. *Thank You, Lord.*

He jolted forward, but the officer held a hand out. "Those are my sons." It wasn't a request, and he didn't wait to hear the officer's response. He ran at a full sprint to the van.

"Daddy," Caleb screamed. The twins let go of each other and held their arms out. They didn't seem injured as the officers on either side of the door stepped back.

James kneeled down. Caleb and Ethan hurdled into his open arms. His hands splayed across their small backs. Their soft cheeks, wet with tears, pressed into his temples.

"Daddy." Ethan's cry mixed with a laugh broke his heart.

"Guess what, Dad? I put on my seat belt all by self," Caleb said, his little voice shaking. "Ethan needed help."

James opened his eyes enough to look into the van. A ripped-up bench seat in the back of the van held three seat belts. The middle of the van had holes on the floor where rows of seats used to reside. He choked back a sob at the provision of safety. "That was very smart of you boys. You're not hurt? Are you sure?"

They shook their heads. Their blond hair brushed against his hair. "Daddy, you saved us, huh?" Ethan nodded his head while he asked. His son's long eyelashes held tiny teardrops.

James closed his eyes. His entire body shook

with emotion. He fisted the backs of their shirts, wishing he could hug them tighter but careful to be gentle. "God did, buddy." The words barely escaped his swollen throat. "And He used our neighbor to help."

James twisted to look over his shoulder at the woman in question. She stood with a hand cupped over her mouth, her head bent. She'd always been attractive, but at the moment, she looked a thousand times more beautiful than he'd ever noticed.

He fought back the habitual onslaught of questions and theories flooding his mind whenever a problem arose. It made him an asset to his company, but as a parent he didn't want to face what his analytical mind shouted: this was too bizarre to be random.

The events of the last week shifted together in his memory, a puzzle begging to be solved. The blood in his veins ran cold. Bottom line: it had to be his fault, and he had no guarantee they wouldn't try again.

TWO

Rachel fought off a relieved sob as she watched James reunite with his sons. His broad shoulders provided enough room to embrace both children at once. He stood as he held them to his chest, their little feet dangling. Both pairs of little arms wrapped around his neck.

She turned to the side, not wanting to intrude on their moment. She'd gotten to know James and the boys as they car-pooled to church together every Sunday and Wednesday...at least until a few days ago when he'd left without her.

Last Sunday, she had walked to the sidewalk at the appointed time and found his car already halfway down the street. She wouldn't have minded driving on her own to church, but the lack of communication infuriated her. She'd half hoped he would explain, but on Wednesday he'd gone without her, as well. She'd meant to talk to James about it the past few days, but the awkwardness of the situation didn't inspire her to make the first move. And now certainly wasn't the time.

Other sirens approached, but they had a different rhythm to them. Her suspicions were confirmed as an ambulance pulled to a stop on the main road. She didn't envy the commuters the traffic jam it created, but his boys were alive. That was all that mattered.

A policeman stepped in front of her. "Ma'am? Were you the one that called in? I need to ask you some questions."

Something flew into the back of her legs. Her knees almost buckled. She looked down to find two three-year-old boys firmly attached to her legs. The officer smiled. "I'll give you a minute," he said.

"Daddy said you saved us." Ethan held on to her right leg.

Caleb squeezed her left knee. "We're supposed to say thank you."

"I didn't say you should tackle her, though."

Rachel twisted her torso to find James McGuire, tears in his eyes, flash a sheepish grin at her. "I—I can't thank you enough," he said.

He reached above the boys and pulled her into an awkward hug. His arms squeezed her tight around her shoulders for half a second, as if he was about to lift her up instead of embrace her. Despite it being a clumsy hug, her cheeks heated. His abrupt release threatened her balance, but the boys' weight around her feet helped steady her. She averted her eyes. She didn't want him to see how his hug affected her.

James cleared his throat and bent down. "Boys, let Rachel move." The twins took the cue and jumped into his arms again. They had blond hair, from what she assumed was their mother's side, but their blue, sparkling eyes and dark eyelashes were an exact duplicate of their father's.

A movement in the distance caught her eye. A man crouched between two trees on the opposite side of the street. The kidnapper returned to the scene to spy on them? A coldness that made no sense in a California suburb chilled her skin. "He's there," she shouted, raising a finger up. She trained her eyes and finger on him, but it seemed he didn't care. He stared right back. A shiver ran down her spine.

The cops immediately responded in pursuit. A second later the man broke eye contact and scaled the closest fence.

"Get him," she whispered.

James straightened, the boys still in his arms. His eyes flicked from the officers in pursuit back to her. She couldn't imagine what he was feeling. Judging by the way the muscles along his chiseled jaw tensed, barely controlled rage was the emotion of the moment.

"Was that a bad man?" Ethan asked.

"Yes." A steely tone radiated off that one word.

Caleb tugged on his collar. "And they're going to put him in jail?"

His chest heaved. "Yes." His voice cracked. "So he can never try to take you away again."

Rachel's ribs constricted. A man like James should never have had to lose his wife or even worry about having to lose his kids. She'd seen the way he parented them at church, during their car-pool rides, and occasionally through her window as they ran around their backyard while the boys giggled and taunted James with cries of "Chase me, Daddy."

Such a man didn't deserve to deal with this kind of fear, the kind she'd experienced most of her life. An inevitable darkness surrounded people like her.

James frowned, snapping her out of the morose thoughts. His dark mop of curls hung low and emphasized his blue-gray eyes. She followed his gaze as paramedics crossed the grass, heading toward them. "Are you hurt?" James asked.

She put a hand on her neck. "Nothing a good

stretch and a visit to the chiropractor won't fix." She reached out and gently touched the twins' blond heads, needing reassurance they were fine.

Two officers approached. "Sir? Ma'am? We need to talk to both of you."

James nodded but his gaze didn't leave her. Two paramedics flanked James. They each talked to the boys in hushed tones as they asked questions and tried to evaluate them. The boys clung even tighter to their father's neck. Their little red T-shirts against his navy-collared shirt gave a resemblance to a superhero.

Rachel inhaled sharply. His gaze always sped up her heart a little. It needed to stop because they could never, ever, be anything more than neighbors.

She turned on her heel and faced the officer. "Of course. Anything you need." The stagnant air, mixed with the smell of diesel and tar from construction, threatened the start of a headache. Her stomach gurgled with hunger pangs, as if jealous for attention.

After a series of endless questions, the beeps from a tow truck backing up halted her train of thought. They were taking her car. The muscles in her back tensed. Transportation meant freedom and control. How long would it take for them to fix the air bag and the transmission she felt certain she'd dropped?

The officer pressed his lips in a firm line, as if impatient. She nodded for him to continue, but she half heard his next question. Her gaze, fueled by a desperate need for proof the kidnapper was gone, swept past the blue uniform. She studied the hedges, flowering bushes and trees surrounding her. She couldn't get past one question the officer hadn't yet asked: Why would the kidnapper return to the scene and spy on them?

James studied the boys in his rearview mirror on the drive back home. Physically they were unharmed and seemed like themselves, but they remained silent, their gazes locked on the blur outside their respective windows. A clear sign that his normally talkative twins weren't fine.

Their mom would've known how to help them cope after the attempted kidnapping. His throat tightened. Nikki had been gone two years. The boys probably didn't even remember the sound of her voice.

He squeezed the steering wheel. Ever since the hit-and-run had taken Nikki away from him, he drove only when absolutely necessary. So much so, his younger brothers had accused him of becoming a hermit, and his mother worried aloud he'd developed agoraphobia. Only his father seemed to understand. Or maybe he didn't. James couldn't tell because he hardly said a word.

The manic chase to the subdivision exit marked the first time he'd driven aggressively since the accident. Thankfully, his neighbor didn't seem to have such squeamishness. He would never forget the way she'd tried to block the van, and then, despite being hit, gone after them like a raging bull.

What was the proper thank-you gift for such an act of selflessness? His throat swelled at the possibility of what could have happened had she not intervened. He gritted his teeth and forced the emotions to take a backseat.

Rachel sat in the passenger seat in silence, her hands squeezed together. He'd insisted on giving her a ride home after her car was towed. It stood to reason she'd be distraught over her banged-up vehicle. Even so, she was uncharacteristically quiet and still. She hadn't let a second go by with silence on all the other rides they'd shared to church and back.

He forced a small smile. "Hey. Are you okay?"

She blinked and jerked in her seat. Her wide eyes roved past James and the boys, as if she'd been awakened from a dream and surprised she wasn't alone. "I don't know." She shrugged. "I mean, I'm sure I will be." Her voice took on a chipper tone. "I suppose it takes a while to process things when something like that happens."

The sudden positive take didn't ring true. "If you hadn't slowed them down…"

She flashed him a dark look and darted a glance behind him. Ah, message received. She didn't think he should discuss it any more in front of the boys.

But James felt the need to talk about it. The squeal of her tires had made him look through the living room window to discover the boys had slipped outside without him. They had asked if they could ride their bikes outside, and he had said they could after his phone call. They were supposed to have waited. He never let them go outside alone.

He shouldn't care what Rachel thought of him, but still wanted to explain so she wouldn't think he was an irresponsible dad.

James groaned inwardly. Discussing their disobedience now would only make the boys think the kidnapping attempt was their fault. How would the experience affect them in the long run?

His pulse ran hot and fast again. Relief turned to anger at the situation. He'd calmed down after the paramedics had checked the twins. His initial reactions began to seem like paranoia. Now he wasn't sure. Could the kidnapping attempt be connected to the anomaly he'd discovered at work or the phone call he'd made two days ago?

"We're going home, right?" Caleb asked.

"Yeah, buddy." That was the third time in two minutes one of the boys had asked. They should've recognized their surroundings since they were gazing out the windows.

"And the bad guys are in jail?"

James's throat tightened. They still hadn't caught the escaped kidnapper, but the officers assured him they would. Patrol cars circled through the area, neighbors were on alert and the cop seemed positive the man wouldn't be foolish enough to try to get at his kids again.

Rachel twisted in her seat. The green tints in her blue eyes sparkled off the rays from the setting sun. Her grin held a hint of mischief. "Do you boys have a favorite food?"

Ethan shouted pizza at the same time Caleb yelled ice cream. Rachel nodded. "Mine, too." She stiffened and faced forward. "I'm not trying to imply we eat together. I just thought a treat might help them get their minds off things."

James shook his head. "I didn't think of that." But the image of her at his dinner table made his lips twitch, almost into a smile. "So you boys want pizza?"

"Yeah," the twins echoed in unison.

She tilted her head back and released a lyrical laugh. She turned to him as her chestnut hair spilled over her right shoulder. "Do you ever get used to them speaking in stereo? I don't think I'd ever be able to get over it. It's amazing."

Warmth filled his chest. "They're something special." Now that his children were out of immediate danger, he registered the soft-shell navy jacket, the white-and-navy blouse, navy pants and navy flats Rachel was wearing. She looked amazing in his favorite color. James jerked his head back at the unbidden thought.

He pulled into his driveway and hit the garage opener out of habit. He frowned at his mistake and shifted into Park. "Sorry. I forgot to stop in front of your house."

She raised an eyebrow. "So I could walk three feet instead of six? No worries." She hopped out of the car before he could reply and waved at the boys. "You have a good night, okay?"

"Bye." They yelled in unison and squirmed forward against their seat belts.

James stilled for a moment, searching for the right words to say as she walked away. Should he invite her to eat with them? Was it too forward? Would she be okay? Having a man point a gun at your face, even through a window, had to be a lot to process. He opened his mouth as he lowered the passenger window, but she'd already disappeared into her house.

He pulled the car inside the garage and allowed the door to drop before releasing the boys. They ran up the steps and through the connecting door into the kitchen as they chatted about pizza and ice cream. For a split second, everything seemed normal again. His neighbor was right. They'd needed a distraction to help them get their mind off the kidnapping attempt.

For him, it was the opposite. Now that he didn't need to put on a brave face for Rachel or the boys, he could concentrate. Sure, there were plenty of creeps roaming the city, but the kidnapping didn't seem random. Why would kidnappers pick a cul-de-sac deep in the heart of the subdivision? The timing of it all seemed suspect. Was his family a target?

He worked at Launch Operations, a space transport company. The anomaly he'd found within the scripts he monitored meant a possible weapon was hidden inside a satellite scheduled to launch. His fingers twitched to call Derrick, his NSA contact, and demand protection. After all, it was Derrick who had asked him to help the NSA in the first place.

Or was James jumping to conclusions, connecting dots that didn't belong together?

He followed the boys inside and found them jumping on the couch. "I was looking forward to pizza, but we could always have vegetable stew instead."

The twins froze, their mouths open, and dropped to their bottoms on the cushions. Ah, his boys may have been through a horrible ordeal, but they were smart enough to test how far this "treat" business went. He melted at their hopeful grins, lowered himself to his knees and hugged them again. When he thought about what might have happened—

"Daddy, are you sad?" Caleb asked.

He shook his head and blinked away the growing moisture. "No, the opposite. I'm very, very thankful for you."

"'Cause Rachel saved us, huh?" Ethan asked, but he was already nodding the answer.

James nodded along and attempted to keep their beautiful neighbor out of his mind. "Yes." Hugging her had been an impulse, and now he wished he'd never discovered her hair smelled like fresh raspberries.

"Listen." He cleared his throat. "I've been thinking Uncle David and Aunt Aria haven't seen you for a long time. What do you think about a visit?"

Their eyes widened, and they let out a whoop, no doubt thinking of the all the toys Aria had brought with her last time. James had never been so thankful he had a good relationship with his brother and sister-in-law. Hopefully they would be available, and if not, he'd just drive to his mom and dad's. He could drop the boys off and drive all night to come back to work. At least then he'd feel safer knowing they were far away until the launch, and the possible threat, was over.

"So," James continued, "I need you to go to your room and pack some clothes in your backpacks just like we did when we went camping on the church trip. Think you can do that?"

"What about the pizza?" Caleb asked.

James's stomach growled at his question, sending the boys into giggles. "What if we picked it up and ate it in the car?"

Their reaction didn't disappoint. They jumped up and cheered. He loved that something so simple as drive-thru food caused so much excitement. They were like their mother that way. She had found joy in the small, everyday things. Their little legs were already in motion, sprinting off to their shared room. "Don't forget clean underwear and socks," he called after them.

His shoulders relaxed. Plans always helped. He picked up his laptop from the end table and flicked it open. *Please show me I'm wrong, Lord. Let this just be a horrible coincidence.*

He'd set up his browser's home page to his work login since he often telecommuted. As a systems administrator, he put in significant overtime and monitored all processes on the servers in the weeks leading up to each launch.

In three days there was yet another telecom satellite scheduled to launch from an air force base his company leased from the government. Mission Control remained at the main offices in the city, but there would also be a small control tower next to the launch site.

James worked around the clock before each and every launch, ensuring there would be no programming glitches. And he'd never found a glitch he couldn't repair. It was fixing a small script error that had alerted him to the abnormality in the first place. Otherwise, he'd probably never have noticed it.

James typed in his username and password. An orange box flashed on the screen. He narrowed his eyes. *User access denied.* He gripped the sides of the monitor. This was confirmation the kidnapping was no coincidence. They were in danger.

He grabbed his cell, dialed Derrick and listened to the phone ring. The wind swept his curls farther down his forehead. The first step would be to close all the windows while he prepped to leave.

He strode to the first window and shoved it closed. Across the small stretch of grass between their houses, all of Rachel's windows were also open.

A man—the same man that'd escaped—crept through the shadows of her living room.

THREE

The wind whipped Rachel's hair forward as she walked to the fridge. She lifted the ponytail holder she often wore as a bracelet and pulled her hair back. Now that she'd changed out of work clothes into her sweatpants, a T-shirt and zippered hoodie, she could attempt to unwind.

She loved this time of year. The gentle winds carried the smell of blooming fruit trees. It soothed her frayed nerves.

She had almost broken her own rule and let her guard down with James. The events of the day had brought back memories and emotions from her childhood she didn't want to face. The entire reason she'd escaped that life and succeeded was that she depended on no one but herself…and God.

The pitiful contents in the fridge caused her stomach to gurgle. Eggs, a soggy bag of salad mix and a half-full container of smoked turkey all served as reminders she needed to run to the grocery store. If only she'd remembered her dinner before the tow truck had left with her car. In the unlikely event insurance didn't declare the car totaled, she'd find herself driving a car that smelled like moldy burrito for weeks.

Inside the freezer, though, she found a treat. An unopened package of cream-cheese-filled jalapeño poppers prompted a grin. She wouldn't have to make eggs, after all. She carried the box to the oven and leaned over to enter the temperature.

Two steel arms pinned her against the stove and took her breath away. She opened her mouth in a silent scream. Her veins pumped hot lava as she struggled to push back.

"If I can't take the kids, it seems you'll do." A scratchy voice filled her right ear. "I'm not leaving empty-handed." The hot breath sent a chill down her spine and overwhelmed her with nausea. Her lungs burned from the lack of oxygen as the man leaned his whole body weight against her. She couldn't turn her head. Her arms were bolted to her sides.

The only thing in her line of vision was the French rolling pin resting on the top of the stove. Her biceps burned, straining to get free.

The man squeezed her tighter around her torso, sending lightning bolts of pain down her spine and legs. She struggled as he growled,

"Now who's sorry she tried to play the hero? Huh?" He shook her body, and her head lashed forward, almost hitting the range hood.

"Guess we'll find out how much your boyfriend loves you, won't we?"

Boyfriend? Was he out of his mind? If it was a drug-induced rage, he would be beyond reasoning. No matter how she strained, she proved no match for the man's strength. Tears blurred her vision and ran down her cheeks. She'd left a life of violence behind, but it'd found her. This was how it would all end?

He lifted, and her feet no longer touched the ground. His tight grip wouldn't allow her lungs to expand. She couldn't scream. Her temples pulsed with a stinging sensation. *Please make it stop!* She didn't have much oxygen left. The hold jogged her memory. Had she gone through a similar exercise in self-defense class?

Rachel clenched her jaw as he stepped back, carrying her away. She swung her feet backward, between his legs, and looped her toes behind his calves. She closed her eyes and locked her knees. She pressed her feet forward. Her muscles burned with the effort.

He growled as he struggled against her legs to take another step. He still maintained his hold, but his arms loosened slightly.

Her toes touched the ground. Rachel took

in a greedy inhale, but there was no time to catch her breath. She twisted her right wrist and raked her knuckles firmly across the top of the man's left hand.

He yelped and released her. Rachel stumbled against the stove and reached for the rolling pin. Tapered on both ends, she gripped the right side. She spun on her heel just as his hand reached her shoulder. She twisted her hips and smashed the side of the rolling pin into his head. He stumbled back but remained upright.

"Help!" Her lungs stung from the effort. Rachel took a step forward and swung the rolling pin again as the man rushed her.

The back door burst open. James filled the doorway.

The diversion shifted her focus, and the man blocked the rolling pin. It flew backward and smacked the edge of her shoulder before it tumbled to the ground.

She cried out. James yelled something she didn't register as the kidnapper snarled and charged at her. Rachel tightened her fist and threw a punch directly to the middle of his chest. The man stumbled back. Pain vibrated up her arm to her throbbing shoulder.

His right hand reached into his jacket and pulled out a jagged knife.

Rachel gasped, paralyzed.

James stepped forward, and his foot whipped out a kick so fast that if Rachel had blinked she would've missed it. The knife soared into the hallway. The man's fist aimed for James's face, but her neighbor sidestepped the punch.

In a seamless motion, James twisted the man's wrist into an odd angle. The man cried out, and James pushed him down until the kidnapper sunk to his knees. He put a foot on his back and pressed him all the way to the ground while gathering the man's other hand.

James sat on his back. "I called the police on my way over here. Do you have any zip ties or rope to help hold him until they arrive?"

Rachel tried to stop shivering, but her body refused. The adrenaline rush took control. She may have attended kickboxing and self-defense classes regularly, but it didn't compare to facing someone wishing to harm her. "I…I might have something."

She ran to the garage and riffled through the few tools she had piled on a card table in the corner. Why didn't she think to have zip ties or rope as part of her tool kit? Her stomach twisted at the shame of not being prepared. She thrust off some of the items on the vinyl tabletop until her fingertips grasped a ball of twine she'd intended to use in preparation for her first raised vegetable garden. It wasn't rope, but it'd have to do.

She dry heaved. Her entire body trembled. This wasn't supposed to happen in a good neighborhood, to a church-going business owner. She'd done everything right, hadn't she? Rachel shook her head, as if forcefully throwing the thoughts away. She ran back into the house.

James accepted the ball, frowned, and tied up the man's wrist and ankles.

The man underneath James's weight grumbled.

"Who sent you?" James asked.

The man went silent. Rachel's pulse quickened. Why would James think someone had sent him? She crossed her arms over her chest, trying to calm her heart rate.

"I asked you a question." James almost spat out the words. His face turned slightly red.

The kidnapper twitched but said nothing.

"Why do you think someone sent him?" she asked, her voice weak.

Grief crossed his features as his eyes, dark and tortured, met hers. "I want to know why they tried to kidnap my kids and then you."

Rachel blinked. "I'm pretty sure he's on meth or something." She recognized the symptoms, and judging by the man's eyes and the pallor of his skin, she imagined he'd spent years addicted to illegal substances. "I doubt you'll get any useful answers from him right now."

The sound of sirens rang through the window screens. "I hope that's for us."

"Should be." James didn't take his eyes off the man underneath him. "I'd hoped they were still in the vicinity. They should've been hunting for this guy."

Her shoulders relaxed, the reality sinking in. James had the man subdued. The police were on their way. Once the man was gone, the danger would be over. Everything could go back to normal. "Thank you, James," she whispered, straining past her aching throat.

She stared at the kidnapper's meaty hands, hands that had almost succeeded in taking her, hurting her. Was this all because she had stopped him from kidnapping the neighbor's kids?

No good deed goes unpunished. Her uncle used to say that often. Of course, he was a drug dealer, and the only good deed he'd ever done was not forcing Rachel into the family business. She'd often wondered if her uncle knew the quote came from the first female ambassador to Italy. If he did, she was sure he'd never have repeated it again. Her uncle didn't believe women were worth much. None of the men in her family did.

Two police cars parked in front of her house, and the officers rushed to her door. Rachel crossed the wooden floor and flung the door open. "He's in here."

Two officers ran to where James sat. James jumped up from his post on the man's back so the officers could take over. The same officer who'd collected her witness account stood just inside her doorway. "I can send for an ambulance."

"No," Rachel replied. She placed a hand on her neck. "I'm okay, really." Or at least she would be.

The police escorted the man in handcuffs out of the house. While the officer questioned Rachel about what had just happened, James stared out the window. His stomach churned, his neck ached…the beginnings of a tension headache. He'd called out to the boys and told them he had to help Rachel and would be right back as he'd run out the back door, but he'd already been away from his boys long enough.

At least he had told them to play in his office behind the secret door just in case it was a ruse to separate him from the boys, but the fact remained he had never left them home alone before. Now, the first time he had—even just to run next door—was the same day someone had tried to take them away. If there were ever an award for Worst Parent…

"I need to go," he said.

The officer stopped midsentence and looked out the window. "You live there?"

James nodded.

The officer's lips flattened before he nodded. "Okay. I think we have what we need for now. You can go," the officer said to James before he offered Rachel a smile. "I think we've got enough evidence to keep them locked up for a long time. Now that we've got both suspects, you can put your minds at ease."

James stiffened.

Rachel's eyes locked on him. She raised her eyebrows and gave a subtle nod. James knew that look. His mom always did that when she wanted him to do something, say something. Problem was, half the time he had no idea what she'd expected.

A small sigh escaped Rachel. "Why would they target the boys and then me?" She looked at James, but the question seemed directed at the officer.

The cop shrugged. "I wish I could tell you definitively. I don't know about the driver, but this man shows the signs of a crystal meth addiction."

"I thought so," Rachel muttered.

How had she known the signs? He made a mental note to ask her, but he needed to call Derrick immediately before things escalated. He'd never got to finish his call when he'd seen the man creep through her living room. The officer and Rachel seemed satisfied with their theory, but it still didn't make sense to him.

Even if one of the kidnappers was addicted to drugs, why would they target his kids and then Rachel? For money? He didn't make enough to warrant attention. There were plenty more affluent parents in the area, and a hairdresser—even a very good one like Rachel—wouldn't make a ton, either.

The officer nodded at both of them. "Have a nice night."

James and Rachel watched the last police cruiser leave the cul-de-sac. Rachel exhaled. One arm cradled her ribs.

"Are you okay? Do you need an ambulance?"

"No, I'll be fine. Only a little bruised up. I didn't feel like I could breathe fully with that man and then the cops stomping around my house."

She shivered and hugged herself, but there wasn't any breeze. The air remained still. Surely she wasn't cold?

She looked down at his bare feet. James shrugged, self-conscious. "I didn't take the time to put my shoes back on when I saw the man in your house."

Rachel stepped closer to him. "I can't thank you enough for stopping him."

His heart beat a little faster. Should he tell her his suspicions? If they came after her once, what was to stop them again? He'd inadvertently put a mark on her. He shook his head. "Don't thank me. I'm not sure you're safe here."

Rachel frowned and looked around for some clue to his statement. "What do you mean I'm not safe? You heard the officer. They got him. They have both of them."

"You told the police he said, 'Let's see how much your boyfriend loves you.'"

Her cheeks flushed. "I don't have a boyfriend," she said. "And, like the officer said, the guy had to be on drugs or something. Nothing he said made sense."

James raked a hand through his curls. She didn't understand the implication. "I hugged you." His voice gruff, he turned to her. "Back there. I hugged you…twice. We held hands."

"We were praying. I was trying to be supportive." Her eyes widened as she held both palms up.

"The kids hugged you," he continued, "while the kidnapper watched. We drove back together. Until Sunday, we had been driving together twice a week."

"About that—"

"I...I think he was referring to me," James said, trying to get to the point. "I'm afraid I put a target on you."

Rachel's breath hitched, but she said nothing. She took a small step back, as if replaying his words in her mind. She frowned, her mouth dropped slightly.

"I'm sorry. I have to get back." He took a step toward her. "Put a bag together with the essentials—clothes, money, whatever you might need to leave for a few days. Meet me at my house, and I'll take you wherever you want. I just don't think you should stay here alone. Please."

Rachel blinked. "I...I don't understand. They caught him."

James blew out a breath. He spent all day talking in computer codes. His communication skills were rusty at best, and he hated it. "I've already left the boys alone long enough." He put his hands on her shoulders, and heat radiated up his arm. He stepped back immediately. "Grab your stuff, and I'll give you a ride to somewhere safe. I'll explain on the way. I promise. And if you still think I'm crazy, I'll pay for you to take a cab back here."

She raised an eyebrow. "Is it possible you might be overreacting? They've caught both men now. He was probably after me because I could identify him, because I messed up their plan." She placed a hand on the back of her neck. Her eyes widened as she looked up at James. "He said, 'If I can't take the kids, it seems you'll do.'" Her gaze stayed on him, but it seemed she was staring into the void. She blinked rapidly and recognition crossed over her features. "Someone is trying to find leverage on you?" She flung a hand to the door. "Why not tell the cops your theory while they were here?"

He blew out a long breath and raised both eyebrows as if accepting bad news. "Because it's not a matter for them. It needs to stay with the NSA."

Her forehead crinkled. "The NSA?"

"National Security Agency." James didn't have time to explain his career history. "I have a contact there that I need to reach before complicating matters by going to the police."

"James." Her voice came out as a plea, soft yet powerful enough to make his stomach flip. "Are you sure?"

He hung his head. "No." He raised his eyes to meet hers. "But do you really want to take the risk I'm wrong? Please close your windows and lock your doors. Get your stuff, and we'll talk at my place."

He turned and left the way he came—out the back door—before she could ask any more questions. He stepped onto the lush grass, grabbed the top of the fence and lifted himself up and over into his own yard.

"You could've used the front door." Her voice reached him through the open windows.

"Close your windows and pack," he hollered back. He slipped the keys out of his pants' pocket, unlocked his back door and went inside.

"Ethan? Caleb?"

"Daddy, can we have pizza now?" Ethan's voice filtered through the secret door.

His shoulders dropped and he smiled. They seemed fine, but for how long? He ran downstairs to hug his boys and tell them it was time to leave.

FOUR

Rachel's home, once a comfort, now seemed empty and full of shadows. Her heart raced. The cops were long gone. The neighborhood grew quiet with only the hum of nearby traffic wafting through the trees.

The NSA? Maybe she didn't know her neighbor as well as she thought. Did she really need to get out her suitcase? Could she ignore him and live with the possibility that he was right?

Another burst of wind through the windows prompted her into action. She'd already locked the front door. Of course, the back door had been locked, but James had made short work of that when he'd burst through to save her.

While grateful, she saw it as a sign that she needed a dead bolt installed on the back door, as well. And without a car, the best she would be able to do in the way of security for the night would be to place a chair underneath the doorknob.

Her hand froze over the kitchen window. How had the kidnapper gotten inside in the first place?

She shoved and locked the windows, going as quickly as she could throughout the house. She stumbled in the hallway to a halt. The kidnapper's knife had gouged her kitchen floor. The reality of what had almost happened made her heart race. Suddenly lounging alone on the couch sounded like the least appealing thing in the world.

She forced herself to continue her walkthrough. In her peripheral vision something seemed off. She placed a hand on the door frame of the bathroom. The window screen had been ripped from top to bottom.

Her breathing quickened. She gulped and took short steps closer to the window. She lifted her chin and leaned forward to see outside. The flowering bushes below the window—something she used to find beautiful—now seemed like nothing more than a place for a man to hide.

Her fingers drifted across the rough edges of the screen. So that was how he'd gotten inside. Had the kidnapper watched her from afar? Seen James drop her off? Seen her laughing with the boys about pizza and ice cream? A shiver ran down her spine. The familiar sensation she'd become all too accustomed to as a child returned—an instinct she'd promised herself she'd never ignore.

She wasn't safe.

She shoved the window closed and ran down the hall. Rachel flung open the coat closet and grabbed a baseball bat. She lunged up the stairs, two steps at a time. She peeked behind each door and underneath her bed before she grabbed a backpack and filled it.

While she'd promised herself she'd never trust or depend on a man, this wasn't the same. James would take her somewhere safe... Although at the moment she couldn't think of a place to go. Surely she would think of somewhere by the time they left.

Five minutes flat and Rachel was ready to leave. She grabbed her purse and slung it diagonally across her torso on her way out the front door. Oh, how she wished her car wasn't out of commission. Her jaw clenched. She should've insisted on a ride to a rental place before coming home, and then she wouldn't have to rely on a man—a man that had a lot of explaining to do.

Rachel opened the front door and peeked behind the bushes lining the porch. The sun hung low in the sky. Pale blues, pinks and violets outlined the clouds. She used to love this time of day, but now it created shadows underneath the trees. Were her eyes playing tricks on her, or were those really just shadows?

She took a deep breath and darted behind the giant oak separating their houses. Squeezing past the lilac bush, she made it to his front patio. With a look over her shoulder, she rang the doorbell.

A shadow crossed the peephole before the front door opened wide. James surveyed the area behind her. "You're fast. Good. Come on in." He'd changed into a soft-looking Henley the color of a night sky, faded jeans and sneakers. She'd never seen him look so…casual. Even on days she knew he worked from home, he at least wore tan pants and a collared shirt. His glance moved to the bat still in her hands.

Her cheeks heated. "You made me nervous." She shook her head. "Well, the kidnapper made me nervous, but you—"

"I get it." He nodded solemnly. "I wasn't critiquing."

Rachel stepped past him into the living room. The warm muted colors on the walls made her think of a cabin in the woods on a fall day. A leather couch, a navy-cloth recliner, a thick wooden coffee table and a big-screen television furnished the living room. A décor fit for an all-male house. "Nice place."

He surveyed the room as if he hadn't noticed. "Thanks, uh, yours was, too. I would've said something but—"

She tried to smile but failed. "You were a little busy."

James closed the door and flipped the dead bolt. "So, have you figured out where to go?"

She blinked. "Where to go?"

"Do you have some family in town you can visit?"

The very word—*family*—caused her jaw to clench. A family man like James probably didn't understand the only reason she counted herself among upstanding citizens was that she'd escaped from her relatives. "Uh, no."

She slipped the bat into the opening in her backpack and crossed her arms. "I need you to tell me what's going on before I decide where you'll drop me off."

"Fair enough." James looked over her head. She turned around to follow his gaze. Through the opening of the curtains she could see a nondescript black sedan pull to a stop. "Do you know anyone who drives a sedan like that?"

"Uh, no."

His eyes narrowed. "I don't, either." James stepped to the intercom panel next to the door and pressed a button. "Boys, game time. Let's see how fast you can get back down to my office. Remember to bring your backpacks. Ready?"

He let go of the button. "Yeah," little voices hollered through the speaker.

James pressed the button. "Set. Go." He crossed over to the bookshelves and put his hands on the middle shelf and pulled. "I have an important phone call to make before we talk." The right side of the bookshelves swung open, revealing a stairway.

Rachel's jaw dropped. "That's the coolest basement door I've ever seen."

The floor vibrated as a herd of elephants approached. Rachel spun around. How such little feet could make so much noise was beyond her comprehension. The boys ran past her and down the stairs.

James looked over his shoulder. "Welcome to my home office."

He watched the look of disbelief cross his neighbor's face. "My brother is a contractor and my sister-in-law is an architect." James reached past her and grabbed his bag "The first time she stepped inside my house she said the ugly brown door in the living room had to go. Aria believes every house should have a hidden door."

He peeked out the windows. "Two men in

suits got out of the sedan and are coming this way. I may be overreacting, but I'd feel a lot better if we both got downstairs before our unexpected visitors ring the doorbell."

Her eyes widened, but she remained silent. James could kick himself. Once again, his inept communication skills were messing things up. He operated in an analytical and efficient fashion while she was clearly a people person, apt to taking her time and discussing all the options—something he'd heard normal people did.

Well, he couldn't take the time to say anything more now. He stepped past her as the boys jumped up and down at the bottom of the steps.

"How fast were we, Daddy?"

"Yeah, how fast?"

James grinned and looked back to see Rachel's face relax, although the lines around her eyes were still tight. "One second, boys. I need to lock the door."

They maneuvered an awkward sidestep. Her arm brushed against his. James almost slowed down from the sudden warmth of her touch.

The back of the swinging bookcase had a regular doorknob. He pulled it closed and flipped the hooked latch on the back to keep anyone else from accessing the entrance. If anyone recognized it as a door, though, they'd be able to break the hook pretty easily. "My sister-in-law asked me if I wanted it to double as a panic room, but I thought that would've been over the top. Now I wish I'd taken her up on it."

Even more so after he heard about the harrowing experience his brother Luke had gone through in the past year. A panic room had saved Luke's life and the life of Gabriella, another new sister-in-law.

Downstairs, they found the boys playing with the train table stationed near his desk.

Rachel turned to him, wide-eyed. "Okay, we're downstairs. Can you tell me what's going on now?"

"Bear with me a little longer." James put one hand on each of the boys' shoulders. "We're going to play another game. There are some men that might try to get into our house. We need to make sure they don't hear us, okay?"

"Are they bad men?" Caleb asked. His fingers tightened around the blue train in his pudgy hand.

James's heart sank. So much for keeping things light and playful. "I don't know. They might be good guys," he answered. "But they're not the men that tried to take you. Those men are in jail."

Ethan didn't respond, but his serious focus on the trains in front of him betrayed his concern.

"So we're playing this game to make sure everyone leaves us alone." Rachel leaned forward and used a higher pitched voice. "Just in case. It's like hide-and-go-seek, and your dad's office is a fort." She flashed a radiant smile and winked at Ethan.

That seemed to calm the boys, and they both maneuvered their trains toward the bridge. James worried his lip. Even at their quietest they still made choo-choo noises without realizing it.

"So, back to what's going on…" Rachel said, her voice hushed. But it came across more like a question.

He straightened and looked around his office with a fresh set of eyes. He'd never had a nonrelative female in his house, let alone his workspace. The framed portrait showed him in front of the South Korean flag as he accepted a black belt. It served as the only wall decoration. His wife had hated that he hadn't smiled for that photograph, but his instructor had told him anything other than a serious face would break tradition. At least his walls weren't white anymore, thanks to his sister-in-law's insistence.

How did he even begin to explain the work predicament to a hairdresser? Nikki had worked in the IT field so James had never had to talk about work to a normal person. In fact, his company discouraged it. He took a deep breath. "You know I work for Launch Operations, right?"

She nodded. "The space company."

"Yes. We launch satellites, usually for telecom services but sometimes for the government, as well."

She raised an eyebrow. "You work on computers there."

"I handle system operations." He searched for the right words. "I watch the processes... the scripts that go through the system. Maybe I should back up—"

Rachel put two hands on her hips and closed her eyes while she inhaled deeply. Her eyes flashed open. "You're trying to dumb it down for me, which I can appreciate, but for the sake of time, why don't you speak candidly? I can ask questions if I need to."

"That works for me." James's shoulders relaxed. "I'm a systems administrator, so I monitor system processes. A glitch happened a few days ago and I fixed it but discovered another process set up for constant monitoring. It sent alerts to someone—I don't know who—on the status of radioactive material."

Her mauve-tinted mouth dropped open. "Radioactive? Is that normal?"

James studied the thin carpet underneath his

sneakers. How much detail should he go into? "For this launch, the radioactive part isn't normal. I had a hunch about what it could mean, though. Do you know what an EMP, an electronic magnetic pulse weapon, is?"

She cocked her head. "Something that could knock out our power?"

"At a rudimentary level."

Rachel darted a glance at the boys. Her frown was so intense her eyebrows almost touched her thick lashes. "You think you found that?"

"The process indicates something radioactive hiding within the satellite, something not on any of the schematics." He blew out a breath. "The launch had been approved. All the necessary permits gathered. The air force even had to certify it beforehand, and it passed with flying colors. There are government officials on site to oversee things, which made me wonder who I could trust."

"That's why you contacted the NSA?"

"A friend of mine, yes. He got back to me a couple days ago and asked me to stall the launch. He said there was reason for concern, but he needed more time to investigate to get to the bottom of it." James sighed. "I agreed to help and wrote a process that writes more processes and sends error messages about the rocket's engine being faulty."

She squinted. "Are you trying to say you wrote a virus?"

James looked at the ceiling. Technically, what he did was different, but he didn't have time to discuss semantics. "Uh, basically. A very complicated virus, if you want to call it that. Bottom line is they won't be able to launch until it's fixed."

"Oh." She blinked rapidly and turned toward his desk. "That's…a lot to take in."

James raked a hand through his hair, the curls off his forehead a moment before they bounced back into position. "I thought the NSA would take over by now. I did my part. But I believe whoever is hiding something on that satellite figured out what I did and shut me out of the system. I got locked out at the same time someone tried to kidnap my kids."

She put a hand on her cheek as she paled.

He hadn't meant to say "kidnap," but the kids didn't react to his slip-up. "That's why," he said, "I think they've been looking for someone to use as leverage against me."

She dropped her hands. "So you'll fix the virus."

James sighed. It was a relief she understood the gravity of the situation and seemed to believe him. He didn't want to explain why the NSA knew it would take other men with the same qualifications days to be able to stop a process James had written. His own parents didn't know the extent of what he had done for the NSA in his younger years.

Crash!

Every muscle stiffened at the sound from above. It sounded like the men broke his back door window to get inside.

"Daddy, I'm scared," Ethan whimpered.

Rachel turned to the boys at the same time as he reached out to hug them. "Your daddy is here, and you're safe." She leveled a cold glare at him. "Now that we know they're not here for a chat, what's the plan?"

He stood and turned the volume on the intercom speaker to low. "They can't hear us, but we can hear them." The basement wasn't sound-proof, but he knew from experience that he would have to be yelling before anyone would hear him upstairs, through the closed door.

He pulled out his smartphone. Telling the police his theories about Launch Operations would be foolish but alerting them to a break-in seemed pretty cut-and-dried. "I'm calling 9-1-1."

Footsteps and doors slamming could be heard even without the aid of the intercom. "I thought they were supposed to be here," a gruff voice said through the speaker.

Rachel's breath hitched.

James turned to make sure she was okay. She seemed to understand his unasked question because she nodded, her lips in a tight line. She crossed her legs, sat on the ground and the boys jumped onto either side of her lap. She whispered into their ears, but he couldn't hear what she was saying. He trusted she was attempting to soothe them as she'd done earlier.

"Maybe they're onto us," the other man said. "I found a car in the garage, but it's empty."

"Or they got picked up by that neighbor girlfriend of his."

James turned in time to see Rachel roll her eyes.

"So we're going to check there, too?" the other man's voice responded. "I heard she's a spitfire."

"I'll go. She won't give me problems."

The other man laughed, a sickening chuckle. "Just because you hide behind your NSA badge."

"Hey," the man yelled. The sound of shuffling feet rattled the bookshelf door upstairs. James flinched. If they were thorough, it wouldn't take them long to figure out there was no wall behind it.

"I wouldn't be here if your team hadn't messed up," the second man said, his voice seething. "So get to work finding the guy's computer. Grab any electronics you see like a hard drive or something."

James glanced at the backpack at his feet where he'd stuffed his laptop. Even if they got their hands on it, he felt sure they wouldn't find anything of use. He'd wiped all evidence of his work from it.

"Trash the place?"

"Whatever it takes to get the job done."

James's heart dropped. He shoved the phone back in his pocket. NSA? This wasn't how the NSA acted, so either the agent was a fake or crooked, but either way, the police wouldn't do him much good if one of the men had an NSA badge to flash.

But now he knew what they were after. They'd confirmed his suspicions. This was about Launch Operations, and Derrick was the only one he could trust. He clicked the intercom volume off before the boys could understand their toys were in danger of being smashed. "I think it's time to go."

Rachel extracted herself to stand. "Where?"

Crash!

James grimaced and swung his backpack over his shoulder. "Let's focus on getting out of here first." He pointed to the white door behind the staircase. "This office used to be part of the garage before we remodeled. Boys, time to go." He led the way in case one of the boys slammed the door open, drawing attention to their location. He cracked the door open and trained his eyes on the set of steps connected to the kitchen.

All clear.

Rachel followed behind.

He waved them closer but kept his eye on the other door into the house. "Remember, no noise, boys. Quiet game."

Rachel placed Caleb in his booster seat while Ethan jumped into his. James shoved the backpacks the boys had discarded underneath their feet.

"We can buckle them in later," she whispered.

James grabbed the seat belt to Ethan's left. That was not a risk he was willing to take, no matter how short the ride. "No. We buckle them in now."

Her wide eyes met his for half a second before she nodded and buckled Caleb.

"Lift the handle as you close it," Rachel whispered, but it came out more like a hiss. Closing the doors still made some noise. James hoped the chaos the men were creating inside would mask their movements.

A moment later they were all inside the Charger. Rachel held her purse against her chest like someone clinging to a flotation device pictured on an airplane safety pamphlet, and her back-pack sat between her feet. "You, too," he said softly, his eyes drifting to the unbuckled seat belt.

She raised her eyebrows and looked at him. Confusion lined her forehead. James shook his own seat belt as he clicked it into place with his left hand.

"Oh." She followed his example as he turned the key in the ignition with his right hand. The door to the house burst open.

"Stop," a man in a black suit hollered. He whipped a gun out from the holster under-neath his suit jacket and aimed the weapon at the windshield.

FIVE

Rachel's heart went into overdrive at the sight of the weapon. Her body stiffened and her fingernails dug deep into the sides of the leather seat. The man kept the gun level at the driver's side of the windshield.

"Shift to Reverse." James spoke out of the corner of his mouth. "While he's focused on me."

He had to be joking. Rachel stared at the gun. One move of the trigger finger and James would be shot. The man took one step down the garage steps, but his weapon remained on target.

The man narrowed his eyes and yelled, "Hands up."

James slowly began to lift his hands. "Rachel." His voice sounded like a plea.

"He's a bad man, Daddy!" one of the boys cried.

The little voice was her undoing. So much

could go wrong, but the alternative meant being in the gunman's control. She'd had more than her share of interactions with arrogant, adrenaline-filled crooks with guns. It never ended well.

Rachel slipped her left hand to the gearshift and shoved it down into Reverse.

The car shot backward. Her head bounced off the headrest as the car smashed against the garage door. The screech of aluminum filled the air as the garage door buckled. James must have floored it.

His hands snatched the steering wheel as the car shot into the street. He swung the car around, and her hands hit the dashboard as he shifted into Drive.

Shards of the left mirror exploded and bounced off the driver's-side window. It mimicked the sound of hail during a thunderstorm. An involuntary scream tore out of her mouth as the wheels squealed and the car sped down the street.

The boys' screeches overpowered hers. "Were you hit?" She turned to find the boys petrified in their booster seats. Little teardrops rolled down their cheeks, but they fell silent. No sign of blood or injury.

James said nothing, but his face paled.

Rachel peeked in the right-side mirror. Were

they still shooting? Two men in suits were running to the black sedan in the cul-de-sac.

She flung her gaze back to James. "Call the police. Have you called the police?"

"I wish we could, but we can't." James zigzagged through the roads out of the subdivision. "Did you hear them? They have fake badges. They shot at us."

She unzipped her purse, hunting for her phone in the unorganized mess. "All the more reason to call." If he wasn't going to do it, she would.

"No. Rachel, we're dealing with people who are trying to launch a weapon in the sky." He sucked in a shaky breath. "Imagine what kind of resources they have at their disposal. I won't trust anyone with the safety of my sons until I hear from Derrick." He lowered his voice so softly she almost didn't hear him continue. "I'd die before I let one of those goons close enough to touch them."

Her fingertips found her phone at the bottom of the bag, but she hesitated to dial. She'd seen firsthand how much he loved his sons and his words only confirmed it. Her finger hovered over the screen. Her heart beat so loudly in her ears she struggled to think straight. "Is Derrick the contact you mentioned? The one from the NSA?"

"Hold on." He took a turn at a diagonal. "Yes. I need to speak with him, and I need to focus now. I'm driving straight to the police station to drop you off, but I'm begging you… Do not bring us into this. Please."

Rachel dropped the phone in her lap. She grabbed the handle on the ceiling and pressed her back into the seat. She needed her bearings. He took another curve. Ah, she knew where they were now. She pointed to her right. "Turn here."

"That'll take me away from the main road."

She looked in the side mirror. So far she didn't see the black sedan in view. That didn't mean much, though. They could be only half a block away. "You want me to wait to call the police? Fine. But we need to do the unexpected. Trust me."

James glanced at her before he turned the wheel at the last second. Rachel's head slammed into his strong shoulder from the momentum.

"Sorry."

She strained to sit upright. "Drive through the community area."

He released an exasperated groan. "There's no road."

Her hands itched to take the wheel herself, to be back in control. "I know. Drive through it. I've sat on that bench and watched teens do it. I called the police, but the point is it can be done." She shoved a hand past his face, pointing. "Dart through there and you can get to a different exit out of the subdivision. They won't see where we went. They won't be able to follow us." She spoke so rapidly she wasn't sure if James caught it all.

James shook his head. "Who's ready for a roller coaster?" he asked drily.

The car dove down the sudden decline and past the basketball court to the left. The whimpers in the back seat morphed into a strange mixture of crying and giggling, as if they didn't know which emotion was called for at the moment.

He didn't decrease the acceleration as they went back up the hill and out onto a new street.

"Take a right," she said. She turned around to get a better view. No sedan in sight. Rachel turned back around. Her stomach roiled as she fought back a sudden rush of motion sickness. "I don't think they saw us."

"Because they don't believe I'm insane."

"Oh, but backing up through a garage door at gunpoint is perfectly reasonable?" Snarky comebacks came naturally, but she'd grown good at holding her tongue...until now. "Sorry. In times like these, instinct is your ally." If only she didn't know it to be true.

He raised an eyebrow. "Sounds like you're speaking from experience."

"Another time." She exhaled, not willing to expound. They reached the main road, and he took a right, barely squeezing between two cars. The final signs of daylight disappeared as streetlights began to glow. Only the remaining light pink hue hung on the western horizon. "Do you know where we're going?"

"Whichever way is fastest to blend into traffic. After that, I'll take you wherever you want."

"Wherever I want?" Rachel couldn't believe he said it with all the nonchalance of a cab driver. "You just told me that those men—possibly part of a terrorist plot—are out to get me, and you're glad to take me wherever I want?"

He darted a glance to the back seat. Rachel cringed. She didn't want to scare the boys but hopefully they didn't know what the word "terrorist" meant.

"I thought that's what you wanted. The police station—"

"I'm sorry. I took it the wrong way. I'm just stressed out. If you think Derrick is the key to safety, I'll wait until you call him."

James shoulders sagged. "I can't apologize enough for getting you involved in this." He turned onto a main drag and headed for the freeway. He merged into the fastest lane and reached into his pocket to pull out his phone.

"Call Derrick," he muttered into the phone's speaker. The phone's rings switched to the car speakers. "Would you mind handing me my Bluetooth in the console? I think it's best this conversation not have an audience." His eyes moved to the rearview mirror to check on the boys.

Rachel found the accessory on top of a small storage container. James hit the turn signal to merge onto the freeway.

"Keep your hands on the wheel," she said. She leaned over and slipped the earpiece over his ear. Her fingertips brushed against light stubble and electricity shot up her arm. She jerked her hands back.

"James?" A deep voice came through the speaker.

James, seemingly unaware of Rachel's response to touching him, reached up and pressed a button on the earpiece. The static sound disappeared from the car speakers. "Derrick," he said. "I've been trying to get a hold of you."

Rachel stared at the earpiece, wishing she could hear the other side of the conversation.

"Daddy, can I have a snack?" Ethan asked. Caleb echoed his brother.

Rachel put a finger over her mouth as James

tried to catch Derrick up to speed. She remembered the lollipops she kept in her purse for after-lunch treats. Admitting she had an addiction to sugar was something she'd yet to do, but she'd found that indulging in one sweet thing after lunch kept her from snacking the rest of the day until dinner.

Normally she'd seek their dad's permission as it was probably past their normal dinnertime, but desperate times called for desperate measures. If James didn't want them to hear Derrick's side of the conversation, he probably didn't want them to focus on the heated words on his end, either.

Their eyes widened and focused on the candy she passed back. "Don't let it spoil your supper, okay?"

They grinned at each other and settled back into their seats to enjoy. *Children are resilient.* She'd heard that so much. But she hated the sentiment. They shouldn't have to be. It was yet another reason she could never be a mother. She didn't ever want children to have to be resilient because of her mistakes, which she felt certain she would make.

How could someone who grew up with such a horrible upbringing ever be a good mother? They couldn't, she told herself for the millionth time. She'd seen plenty of examples, and she refused to become another case study of evidence.

James finished explaining what had happened in the past few hours.

Derrick was silent for a moment. "No, you're right. I don't think this was random."

"I agreed to help, Derrick, under the assumption we'd be taken care of. Now my family and my neighbor are in a…compromising position." His jaw clenched. They weren't the words he'd normally choose, but he floundered to find something suitable, with the boys as an audience, instead of words like *kidnap*, *danger*, *guns* and *kill*. "What do we do now?"

Derrick's sigh on the other side of the line sounded more like a muzzled growl. "You know this wasn't part of the plan, James. I either have a mole inside the agency or someone impersonating an agent. Either way, we need to find out who is calling the shots."

James glanced in the rearview mirror. His gut lurched. A black sedan three cars back changed lanes. Another one six cars back stayed in his lane.

He hadn't taken the time to figure out what the model was when he'd looked out his home window, especially since it had been growing dark. The Charger's automatic headlights flipped on as if in reply. "Derrick, straight up, I'm not interested in how you handle the case on your end. I'm calling because I want to know my neighbor and my kids are going to sleep safe and sound tonight. Is it safe for me to take Rachel to a friend's house? I can get the boys to my brother's tonight. Once I know they're away from any threat, I'll come back and do whatever you need."

"Which brother?"

"The one in Oregon. You remember David and Aria." James flinched at the memory. Right after Nikki's funeral, David had come to stay with James for what he'd called "the transition." Derrick and his wife, Cynthia, had arrived with dinner just as James lashed out at David for calling it such a thing. How could you ever transition from being with the woman you loved to living life with her gone…forever?

"Hold off on that," Derrick said, snapping him back to the present. "The reason I told you how I'm handling the case is in hopes you'd understand I can't offer you protection at the drop of a hat. I need to pinpoint those I can trust and discover how far this goes. Offering you security in Oregon would take some time. And as far as your neighbor, I can't guarantee they won't continue to target her until I gather more intel. For now, I need you to stick together."

James glanced at Rachel. She watched him, her eyes moist with emotion. Knots ached behind his shoulder blades. How could he tell her they had nowhere to go?

He checked the mirrors and switched lanes to take the next exit. Logically, he needed to identify if he did have a tail while Derrick was on the line. "What do you suggest I do, Derrick?" Everything had spun out of his control. Nothing but dead air answered for a full half minute. "Are you still there?"

"Yeah, I needed a moment to think," Derrick finally said. "I need an hour to get a safe house and protection set up. Can you stay low while I do that?"

He took the exit to the right. "An hour?" He pulled up to the stoplight, switched the turn clicker to the left. One black sedan sat two cars back, but no signal blinked on either side. There wasn't an option to go straight. Was one or both of them tailing him?

Rachel's chin jutted forward, her eyes wide. "An hour?" Her whisper sounded incredulous.

"I can't stay put," James continued. "I'm driving on the freeway hoping to blend into traffic." And stay away from black sedans.

"I understand, but I'm doing the best I can with limited resources. I need to do this right,

James. For your own sake and those boys of yours. Surely you can see that."

James did, but he wasn't satisfied with the answer.

"Listen," Derrick continued, "find someplace where you feel safe and sit tight for an hour. You still know how to check for a tail, I assume. I'll contact you in sixty minutes, hopefully with some good news."

"I don't know where—"

"I'm sure you can think of somewhere. Choose somewhere unexpected where your boys feel safe. Gotta go."

"Derr—" A dial tone met his objection. He glanced to the side at Rachel, who stared at him with eager eyes. "Okay, I agree. Sounds good. See you in sixty minutes," he said for her benefit then clicked off the button on his ear.

"He hung up on you, huh?"

If the situation weren't slightly embarrassing, James might've laughed. He found it amusing that Rachel occasionally made statements that sounded like questions in the same way his sons did. She even nodded along like they did. It seemed like a handler's technique to get you to agree. "Well, if you heard, you know what he said."

"Only the last bit." Her eyes narrowed. "You know how to check for a tail?"

James sighed. *Thanks, Derrick.* You'd think a NSA agent would learn to lower his voice over cell phones. "Thanks to television, doesn't everyone?" It served as the most evasive answer he'd given in the past three years, ever since he had left the NSA. "You were right, though. They were looking for someone to use as leverage."

The light turned green. He swung the Charger around the bend and moved immediately to the left-turning lane to get back on the freeway. Horns honked behind him. Rachel leaned over to look out the side mirrors. "Black sedan," she muttered. "Two of them."

James gunned it through a yellow turn light and merged back onto the freeway. "Make sure their seat belts are on correctly."

Rachel gulped. "They are," she whispered.

He checked his mirror. The traffic wasn't as thick heading west, but it wasn't light, either. It'd been years since he trained in driving techniques and even then it was a mere overview. No one at the NSA had expected him to be anywhere but a computer. He shifted the car and passed the registered speed limit. The sedans merged in the lanes behind him.

Semitrucks dominated the lanes ahead of him. He stepped on the speed. The moment he passed one truck, he changed lanes until he was right in front of it and behind another. He flicked his gaze to each mirror. The black sedans were approaching fast on either side. Up ahead to the right was another semitruck.

"They're gaining on us," Rachel said.

James didn't respond. If he lost his concentration, he feared he'd make a costly mistake. The truck behind him turned on the right-turn signal, forcing his hand. Being sandwiched in between two big rigs made it hard to see the traffic signs, but to the right he caught a glimpse. The second street exit was in half a mile. His mind ran through math calculations in a half second. At seventy miles an hour it'd take him four-tenths of a minute to get there.

"Hang on," he mumbled. James pulled up to the bumper of the semitruck in front of him. He crossed into the left lane, zoomed past the semi and glided back into the lane at such a small margin the semi behind him laid on the horn, but James had already crossed into the next lane, sandwiched between two other semitrucks. They were passing the exit. He cranked the wheel. The tires against the ridges in the asphalt made a horrible noise, as he was on the outer edge of the road.

Rachel gasped. Horns honked, but there wasn't the telltale sound of steel crunching. No accidents, but the sedans hadn't been able to follow them. They'd missed the exit. "You did it." Rachel shook her head. "No way you learned to drive like that from TV."

"We're not out of the woods yet." James took a left then three right turns to make sure no one else was following him.

"Do you know where we'll go?" Rachel asked.

"I don't know about you, but the boys and I are going to start eating these seat cushions if we don't get some food soon. I've got some dried fruit in a snack container in the console to hold us until we get some dinner." Speaking of the boys…they were quiet. They hadn't even commented or acted scared during his crazy driving. Something was up. In the dim twilight, he squinted to make out the boys eagerly sucking on white sticks.

He groaned. He took back the thought of something finally going right. "Oh, Rachel. What have you done?"

"What?" She looked behind her shoulder at the boys. "The lollipops?"

"Real terror is twins on a sugar high followed by a sugar crash." He tried to grin, but only half of his mouth cooperated in his attempt to lighten the mood. Adrenaline still rushed through his veins at so many near misses.

Rachel's mouth formed a soft *o*. "I'm sure they're no worse than when I get hungry." She worried her forehead and tapped her fingernail onto her lips, clearly in deep thought. "Somewhere unexpected," she murmured.

Assuming he had lost the cars behind him, what they really needed was somewhere the boys would feel comfortable, somewhere they could weather the sugar high and crash while he got them some food… He turned around. "You've given me an idea of where we can go until Derrick calls."

Five minutes later he turned into the empty parking lot of their church.

Rachel nodded. "Unexpected and yet fitting."

"I'll need your help to hide the car." He pulled to the farthest corner of the parking lot next to a nondescript aluminum shed. "We can remove the lawnmowers and hide them in the bushes behind it."

"Then move the car into the shed. Smart idea. Think it'll fit?"

"It's going to be tight."

"James, I only have a key to the building."

He shrugged. "I'm the deacon overseeing maintenance and youth. I have keys to the shed. And I'll take responsibility if anything happens."

They each grabbed a lawn mower and pulled it into hiding while the boys crunched down on the remainder of the lollipops. As James pulled the car into the unlit space, he silently prayed that hiding the car was a good idea. If the men found them in the church, with the car locked up in the shed, it'd be that much harder to escape.

The last bits of twilight faded into the night. Rachel moved without his direction as she hoisted Caleb onto her hip. He did the same with Ethan and locked the padlock to the shed.

They moved as a team, the children silent, to the back entrance. Rachel slipped her church key from her purse and unlocked the glass door. They stepped in and the door closed behind them with the aid of the automatic hydraulic arm.

Rachel whispered a prayer into the darkness. "Please protect us."

SIX

The dim light from outside outlined a path on the commercial carpet underneath her feet. Rachel turned the corner to walk into the heart of the building. An exit sign at the far end of the darkened hall glowed green. She inhaled the church smell: a mixture of old books, candles, oiled wood and a pine-scented cleaner. The combination was oddly soothing, maybe because on weeks she couldn't give up her anxiety, once she worshipped, she left feeling lighter.

Today won the all-time anxiety award, though. It even beat the time a drug dealer had swung a gun on her uncle and demanded a larger percentage of the profits. Rachel had hidden underneath a bed until one of her uncle's men killed the dealer.

Rachel stiffened. It did no good to replay a past she couldn't fix. She worked hard to focus on positives throughout the day. When her clients started in on a rant or venting, which it seemed ninety-nine percent of her customers enjoyed, Rachel pulled out her favorite heart-warming or humorous story of the week she'd find on the internet. Sometimes she borrowed whatever anecdote the preacher used on Sunday. The other hairstylists teased her for it, but as Rachel reminded them, at least she changed the story each week.

"One second," James said. "I need to make sure the doors are locked."

The soothing feelings of being inside the church dissipated in a heartbeat. Despite the thick walls surrounding her, someone was still on the hunt for them. She couldn't truly let down her guard yet.

Caleb's little hands went around her neck. He twisted in her arms and laid his cheek against her shoulder. His fine blond hair smelled like apple blossoms. He didn't wiggle, he didn't squirm…he trusted his safety in her arms. Rachel's throat swelled, and it hurt to swallow. Or maybe the little guy just found the same comfort she did in the church. She blinked back the emotion. Yes. That had to be why.

Nearing the next corner she twisted to see James over Caleb's head. "Where to?"

"The youth wing," he answered. "There's a room without windows. I filled the fridge for youth night snacks. The boys can play and eat. No one will have a problem if I replenish the stock later."

Meaning he paid for it. Rachel had never heard the man brag, but she knew that James went above and beyond in serving. Was it because he genuinely wanted to or did James have to stay busy to stop from thinking about his wife?

He passed her in the hall, but not before she caught a whiff of citrus aftershave complete with herbal and cedar notes. She followed the outline of his form until he stopped at a corner and stepped into what she presumed must be the youth room. He flipped a switch.

"Cover your eyes a moment," she warned Caleb. He curled into her neck without argument as she closed her own eyes waiting for her pupils to adjust slightly to the light before she opened them. "Okay. You shouldn't get a headache now if you open."

He popped up to a sitting position in her arms. Rows and rows of couches, all in varying degrees of decay, filled the room. Each couch had either sagging cushions, ripped upholstery or more throw pillows than she could count. Caleb's legs wiggled. She grinned. "You know where you are, don't you?"

The moment his feet touched ground, Caleb's

little sneakers ran after his dad. "Dad, can we have Popsicles?"

Ethan bucked against James's arms until he also joined Caleb on the ground.

"No, not tonight. What about mini calzones?"

Rachel's stomach gurgled.

Caleb giggled and grabbed his own belly. "Rar," he growled. "Your tummy needs food," he said, nodding authoritatively.

James turned, his face apologetic.

She laughed. "He's not wrong."

He pointed to a small kitchenette behind her. Six round portable tables and folding chairs fit on the tiled area of the room. He crossed to the three cabinets and opened the middle one. Inside he found paper plates, plastic cups and napkins. "It's not gourmet, but I thought microwaved mini calzones might hold us over until we can make something a little more substantial."

"If you're worried about me, don't. I had planned a menu of junk food tonight." She crossed back to the doorway they'd entered. Having the entrance to the room wide open seemed like an unnecessary vulnerability. If someone had followed them she wanted as many warnings as possible. She kicked the doorstop out of the way and closed the brown door, even though it was without a lock.

He raised an eyebrow but turned back to the kitchenette. "I thought you cooked." He opened the freezer and pulled out the bag of mini calzones. He hadn't exaggerated. Popsicles, ice cream bars, chicken nuggets and frozen pizzas took every inch of the freezer. They would barely make a dent.

The boys giggled so loud she almost didn't answer. They jumped from one couch to the next in a race to the back of the room. "I do cook but not every night…usually on weekends. It's not very fun being on my feet after a full day."

James set the microwave timer and watched it count down. He turned to the clock on the wall. "I thought all our extra turns and side roads took up more time than that. Thirty-five minutes to go until Derrick calls." His shoulders dropped. "The launch is scheduled very soon. Whatever happens, this can't go on long."

She shrugged. What else was there to say? He pulled out the first plate and called the boys while he microwaved a second plate filled with food. The boys found a seat and sat expectantly. James sliced the calzones in two. "Okay. Five each. Remember to blow."

The boys each took a giant breath before aiming a blast of air at their calzones. Marinara sauce splattered to the edge of the plate. Her stomach rumbled again. She'd lost out on the burrito, and her cream-cheese jalapeño poppers were still sitting on top of her stove at home.

James watched her with a bemused smile. "You said you don't have family here. Where do they live?"

The humor she'd felt a moment ago disappeared into a vacuum. "No family. I moved here a year ago." To get away from her family, in fact, but he didn't need to know that so she went on the defensive. "And my friends...well, I think of my colleagues as friends, but really I don't know anyone well enough that I'd feel comfortable crashing at their house."

James turned his eyes onto the microwave. "Really? That's surprising."

She tilted her head. The tone of disbelief bothered her, but she wasn't sure why.

"You seem like the type to have lots of friends," he said.

Did she? A roster of names instantly came to mind. She enjoyed attending movies, parties, concerts and church with them, but she never called them when she was upset or when she needed something. She furrowed her brow. Did that mean they were all shallow friendships?

"I think Derrick is going to give us two options," James said. "We'll each get a protection detail, or he'll send us to a safe house. I'm hoping for the first option so you have a chance to go somewhere you feel comfortable."

His words made sense, but something about the way he was attacking the situation bothered her. Her breathing sped up, but she couldn't put a finger on what bothered her about it. "Like I said, I moved here a year ago. I'm not comfortable calling anyone for something like this," she answered. "I wouldn't want to put them in danger."

Her leaned back and crossed his arms over his chest. "I can understand that. What about a hotel? Think a hotel would let me prepay without a credit card?"

She didn't need to owe him any favors so letting him pay for the hotel was not an option. Except, the last thing she needed was to be spending money not in her budget. "My first choice would be my salon," she said. "I have a couch, computer and minifridge in my office. Everything a girl could need. Plus, it's in a well-lit area of town. If they assign me protection, I'd be fine there."

"Really?" He narrowed his eyes. "But is your name associated with the salon? That'd be like a neon target."

"No. It's associated with a limited liability company. So…I think it's safe. Besides," she finally said, "the building I'm leasing has an alarm system, and there's a twenty-four-hour dry cleaner right next to me. I think I'd be okay."

"You're not taking in account the power of an internet search. I could easily find out you set up the LLC. Your name has to be out there to build your clientele." He inhaled deeply, pressing his shoulders back. "We'll have to find another solution," he said.

She opened her mouth to argue that most people weren't him, but he probably knew better the type of men they were up against so she nodded, hoping that put his personal questions at rest.

He pulled out their food. "So absolutely no family?"

Rachel's shoulders sagged. She should've known he wouldn't let it go. James was an analytical, efficient guy that never started anything he didn't intend to finish...which reminded her. "Hey, why did you leave me high and dry this week?"

His chin pulled back, as if surprised by the question.

"When you went to church without me," she clarified.

"Oh...that." He split the heated calzones onto two plates. "People thought we were dating."

Heat flooded her cheeks. "What?"

* * *

James placed a calzone straight into his mouth—partly to buy himself some time to collect his thoughts—and he couldn't wait any longer to eat something. The sauce was unfortunately at molten-lava temperature. He opened his mouth. "Hot."

His pain didn't dissuade Rachel. "Yeah. I'm pretty sure you knew that would burn your mouth. Bad stall technique. Back to the dating?" Her hands were on her hips, her blue eyes wide and the chestnut hair from her ponytail draped lazily over her left shoulder.

He shrugged. "I thought you knew. When I first suggested you should ride with us, it just seemed the right thing to do, the neighborly thing to do. You had been a regular attender, we were neighbors, it'd save gas, be better for the environment—"

"Are you saying that driving together is what the kidnap—" She shot a glance to the boys who happily devoured their meal while they forecasted who would win their next couch jump contest. "You think that's why the man who came into my house said we were an item?"

He shrugged. "I'm afraid it might've contributed."

She dropped her hands from her defensive

stance and blinked several times as if digesting the idea. She took a step forward and accepted the plate of food while he poured them each a plastic cup of root beer. "I'm still not following. Why did you stop taking me to church all of a sudden? Is it because you knew this might happen?"

"No, of course not." He sighed, wishing he didn't need to explain himself. "Last week I overheard that new guy—"

"Carl."

"Yeah, the one you've been dating. I heard him tell you he wanted to start giving you rides."

Rachel cringed. "Dating? We went on one date. And he did say that, but did you eavesdrop on the rest of the conversation?"

His jaw tensed at her tone. "I hardly call being in the lobby of the church with a coffee eavesdropping. Half of the people in the room likely heard. And, no, I didn't hear the rest of the conversation."

She flushed. "Just because he asked me didn't mean I'd automatically say yes."

He held his hands out. "You're dating him, so I assumed—"

"Again, not dating him. It was one dinner. And since when do you assume something like that? I'm not trying to be rude, but I've never known you to do that." She tilted her head, confusion creasing her forehead.

He pulled back. "I've been told I don't always pick up on signals very well."

"By whom?" she pressed.

Every woman in his life flashed through his thoughts. That probably wouldn't be a helpful thing to say, though. "My mom pointed out that two single people driving to church together would give the appearance of dating." He waved a hand between them.

She pulled her chin back and curled her lip. "You went to your mom about this?" Her tone belayed her disbelief.

"No, I didn't go to my mom about this." He mimicked her tone. "I happened to mention on one of our Sunday phone calls that I was carpooling with my neighbor to church."

She cocked her head and her eyes softened. "You talk to your mom every Sunday?"

"Studies show it improves your health if you talk to your mom once a week. I have my theories about why, but—"

"Okay, but back up." She shook her head. "For the record, I like that you don't make assumptions. I really do. Before now I thought of you as a 'what you see is what you get' kind of guy. You've always been a straight shooter, at least with me. It's refreshing and why I said yes to car-pooling with you in the first place. So I'm sure your mom meant well, but I don't see why that should change just because you overheard—"

The end of her sentence didn't register. She liked he was a straight shooter? It surprised him. No female had ever appreciated that about him. Why did she? Because she liked him or, rather, liked that he felt safe? It was ridiculous to think she'd consider falling for a guy like him, a guy with a ready-made family.

His thoughts shifted to her wondering why things should change. *Because I've never been so drawn to you before, that's why. I feel a jolt of attraction every time I look at you.* He moved his focus to the bubbles on top of his soda and retuned his mind to what she was saying.

"Just because I went on one date with Carl," Rachel continued, "doesn't mean he gets to decide how I get to church and back. Besides, I didn't like how possessive he was acting, and we never had date number two. So, it's a moot point."

James raised an eyebrow. She ended it because the guy wanted her to stop car-pooling?

"What?" Rachel asked.

He shook his head and picked up another calzone, gauging if it had cooled down enough yet.

"A raised eyebrow says it's something."

He chuckled. "Who's reading into signals now?"

She blushed and rolled her eyes. "Face expressions are different. Besides, unlike you, I've always read into people. Not that it's something I'm proud of—I have my own weaknesses—but at least I'm consistent. Let's keep the focus where it belongs, shall we?" She flashed a mischievous smile. "On you."

He snickered. If only she weren't so cute when she got flustered.

"Why the raised eyebrow?" Rachel pressed.

He blew out a large breath, searching for the right words. "It's not that out of the ordinary that a date doesn't want you riding alone with another single man…or any man, for that matter."

Her mouth dropped open, no doubt to object. He held up a hand. "Not that we are ever alone," he amended with a wave to the boys, who grinned. "And I understand, in your view, that I shouldn't even be considered a threat. But, we are roughly the same age and neighbors, so I could see his point."

She pursed her lips a moment. "If it's the right guy—and I can tell you this guy wasn't—but if it was Mr. Right then it stands to reason I would tell you we should stop car-pooling because I'd want an excuse to spend more time with the guy. Correct?"

He mulled over her hypothetical and hated the way his neck tingled in jealousy. But, overall, he could see her point. He nodded. "Fair enough. I just thought you were getting serious about this one and didn't want to stand in the way." She crossed her arms over her chest, and James could feel her disapproval radiating. "Let me amend that," he said. "What I meant was, I didn't want you to feel we needed an awkward conversation—"

Her face erupted in a gigantic smile. "You mean like this one?"

He took a swig of his soda in hopes the cool liquid would cool his reddening neck. "Yeah, like this one."

She smiled and picked up a calzone. "All I'm asking is that you talk to me next time, James."

For a split second he froze. She'd never said his name that way, soft and caring. He averted his eyes but nodded in agreement. His insides heated. They ate standing up, at the counter, in silence for a few minutes. The squeaking springs, from the boys on the couch cushions, accompanied their chewing. For a moment, the briefest of moments, he felt almost normal. The ticking clock on the far wall grated his nerves.

Would there even be a next time? Would Derrick come through for him?

"Do we stand a chance if there are crooked NSA agents after us?" Rachel asked, her voice almost a whisper.

He didn't want to think about the odds if they were being targeted from the inside of the NSA. Besides, the likelihood seemed slim. "We do with Derrick," he finally said.

"Why do you trust him so much?"

James wiped up some escaped sauce with the mini calzone. "The NSA had—maybe they still do—a high school summer intern program. Nikki and I both worked for Derrick straight out of high school. We continued working for him during summer breaks while we attended college at MIT."

Her mouth dropped into that small *o* again that made him grin. "So she must have had the same genius status as you." She set her food down and crossed her arms.

"I can't stand the connotations of that word."

She picked up her cup. "Which are what?"

"Like a superhero of intelligence instead of someone with huge weaknesses like everyone else. Nikki and I both excelled at math, but even within the field, we had strengths in different areas." He shrugged. "Anyway, Derrick served as our supervisor in DC before he moved here."

"So you worked for him after college, too?"

"For a short time." And that was his cue to change the subject.

He pulled his phone out of his pocket and looked at the time. Three minutes until they should get a phone call. The bars at the top were all empty except the shortest one. He groaned. "I forgot. Ever since we installed energy-efficient windows and new roofing on the building, you can barely get a signal."

He threw a thumb over his shoulder. "The boys should be hitting their sugar crash any minute. The youth pastor has a smaller room he uses for counseling or keeping his kids busy while he works." He pointed to the door at the far end of the room. "It has a TV and an ancient VCR—if you can believe that—plus a nice couch. Do you mind trying to wind them down with a video while I use the landline in the office?"

Rachel regarded him with wide eyes but smiled softly. "No problem."

James weaved his way through the dark hallways on autopilot. Thanks to all the hours he'd spent here, it was like a second home. The people at the church had been a lifeline when Nikki had passed, and a year ago, when he'd finally found his footing again, he wanted to give back. The boys loved joining him while he did it.

He opened the dark brown door separating the children's wing from the rest of the building. The main sanctuary and offices were significantly older. A second signal flickered to life on his phone. "Come on, Derrick," he whispered. "Where are you?"

He stepped into the church office and picked up the black receiver. He pressed the button for an outside line. The sound of shattering glass filtered through the hallways and doors of the church.

James dropped the receiver and sprinted down the hallway. He shoved past the door and rounded the corner when he heard Rachel. Her voice, strong and powerful, bit out each word as a command. "You will not lay a hand on those boys."

His bones chilled and his muscles twitched, ready to attack, but surprise was his only weapon. He dared a peek around the final corner. Rachel stood in the doorway of the youth center holding what looked like a knife. She was the only thing standing between his boys and the two men from his house.

SEVEN

Rachel drew a ragged breath. Her core grew hot as if filling with lava. She'd had just enough time to settle the boys with a cartoon when she had heard the breaking glass. She'd told them not to open the door for anyone but her or their dad. They had nodded without moving as she'd locked the door from the inside and run for the entrance to the youth room. She'd unzipped her purse, slung diagonally across her body, grasping for anything that might help. She had barely made it to the open door to block the men's entrance.

Rachel held a wide stance, three feet from the men on the other side of the threshold. In one fist, she gripped her haircutting shears. It was the only weapon she could think of in the heat of the moment. In the other fist, her fingers concealed a travel-size aerosol hairspray.

The gunman to her left held a gun at his right side. If she kicked the weapon out of his hand like James had done at her house… Even if a gunshot released, it'd be impossible to hit the room the boys were in.

The man's sinewy forearms gave her pause. "Where is he?"

"He went to get help," she answered. Hopefully, James had reached Derrick and the cavalry would arrive any second. The second man didn't point a gun at her, but judging by the bulge underneath his jacket, the likelihood he carried one seemed strong. Several white, plastic ends stuck out from his pocket. Could it be zip ties?

He followed her gaze and the man's lips twisted in a smug grin. "Look, lady, let us get the boys, and we'll leave you alone. We won't hurt them."

The gunman gestured the gun to the right, as if telling her to get out of the way. A calm strength she'd never known draped over her trembling arms and fingers. "Maybe you didn't hear me the first time. You will not touch those boys."

Something caught her peripheral vision. A hint of dark, wavy hair? The only light in the hallway came from behind her back. It could've just been wishful thinking, shadows or her eyes playing tricks. She didn't want to look again and take the chance the men would see him. *Please let it be James.*

"See we've got ourselves a problem, then, because I'm not leaving without those boys," the man to the left grunted. "It'd be a shame if I had to hurt you in the process."

"Wh-what if I let you take me instead?" She pulled her shoulders back and forced her chin up, hopeful she came across as confident. "The first set of kidnappers thought I was worth something."

The gunman glanced at his partner. The distraction was enough to peek. James slid slowly around the corner and nodded. He was going to try to take them down, she was sure of it. But with a gun in play, he wouldn't stand a chance.

"See, what you're not getting is we call the shots," the man responded. "I have the gun. What if I want to take all of you? I'm trying to do you a favor and not shoot you, so put the scissors down and step aside."

Rachel gulped and took a step closer to him.

The gunman squinted as if unsure she was threatening or trying to cooperate. He looked down at the scissors in her hand.

"Watch it," the other man shouted. He had his hands outstretched, his focus also on her scissors, ready to grab. Rachel twisted her right wrist, flicked her index finger on top of the aerosol can and pressed down. The spray hissed and hit her mark—the gunman's eyes. He yelled and moved both of his hands upward toward his face.

Rachel grabbed his arm and used the force of her twist to slam his elbow into the door frame. His arm bounced off the wood, but the gun was still in his hand. She shoved her entire body into his arm. His forearm smashed into the door frame as she pressed his wrist past the frame, backward. He loosened the grip on the gun and dropped it.

She kicked the weapon away, into the room, and hopped back to retrieve it. She wanted to be as far away as possible from the growling man. She straightened and aimed the gun at him. His entire face turned beet-red as he wiped at his squinting eyes with his forearms.

Next to him, the other man dropped to his knees with one arm behind him—the same technique James had used on the kidnapper at her house.

"He has a gun," Rachel called out. "On his left side."

James's eyes flicked to hers in recognition as he twisted the man's right arm back. He shoved the guy onto his stomach on the ground and retrieved the gun.

"I think he has zip ties in his left pocket."

James lifted his eyebrows. "How thoughtful." He slipped the retrieved gun into the back of his waistband before moving to the zip ties. He tied the man's hands and feet together within two minutes.

The other guy, blinking rapidly against his teary eyes, sneered. His rage evident by the way he looked at Rachel, she feared he might charge at her. She tightened her grip on the gun and took a step back. He wouldn't be as easy to take down.

"Put your hands behind your back," Rachel ordered.

The gunman leered but didn't respond.

She waved the gun in the same manner he had moments ago. "I know my way around a—" She twisted the gun to the right and left. "SIG-Sauer 9 millimeter?"

He raised an eyebrow. James took advantage of the distraction and kneed the back of his leg. The man dropped slightly but not before he jerked his elbow back toward James.

James twisted at the last moment, barely missing the blow. The man spun around, ready to attack. James faked a punch toward the man's face, but the moment the guy tried to block him, James punched him in the stomach. The man bent over, grunting as James grabbed his wrist and twisted it behind his back. The man's hands were zip-tied behind his back before Rachel could blink.

"Get the boys," James yelled.

She jogged across the room as she checked the safety and shoved the gun into her purse. She slipped the scissors back into their protective case and zipped them inside a compartment. The can of hairspray was somewhere in the room, but she didn't take the time to retrieve it. She knocked on the door. "Boys?" She tried to lighten her voice. "It's Rachel. Let me in."

She waited a few seconds. Nothing. She knocked again, this time harder, and jiggled the doorknob. "Boys? Ethan? Caleb? You don't have to turn the video off, just let me in."

Her heart raced. Were they just too scared to open the door? Had something happened? She riffled through her purse until she found a bobby pin. She bent it open to access the skinniest end. She slipped it into the small hole at the center of the doorknob and wiggled it until she heard a satisfying click.

Rachel flung the door open as James ran across the youth room. "What's taking so long?" he asked.

"I don't know." Her voice shook. The moment she laid eyes on the boys, both curled up on the couch, sound asleep, her shoulders relaxed. An uncharacteristic laugh escaped. "They're asleep."

She put a hand on her mouth to stop herself from crying in relief. The twins had no idea what had just happened. They rested together, safe and cozy on the suede-brown love seat.

James placed his hands on his hips and shook his head. "I've never been so thankful for a sugar crash." He strode across the room. "We need to hurry. I dragged the gunmen into the men's bathroom and barricaded the door with a chair, but I don't know how long that's going to last. They're tied up but not paralyzed."

She lifted Caleb into her arms.

James headed for the door, a quick look over his shoulder. Ethan rested against his chest, not even stirring. "You good?"

She nodded. "I'll be better once we're somewhere safe. What happened to Derrick? Is he still coming?"

"I wish I had an answer. Can you run with Caleb?"

She shrugged. She'd never run before with a thirty-pound weight on her chest. "I'm willing to find out."

James's arms vibrated. He tried to stop the shaking by tightening his muscles, but that only worked against him. He wrapped the fingers around the steering wheel and checked the rear-view mirror for the twentieth time in two minutes. His boys were still fast asleep as he sped through the streets in the darkened night.

Stomach acid rose in his throat. He replayed the events. Had the guys escaped the zip ties yet? Every fatherly instinct had tempted him to kill the men to keep them from chasing after his sons again. What would stop them otherwise? Derrick had let him down again. *I did the right thing, Lord. I'm leaving justice to You.*

Except, would he be able to handle the Lord's timing and version of justice? He'd let Nikki die in a hit-and-run, and the authorities never had found the driver responsible for killing her. The concave spot underneath his Adam's apple hurt from the combination of acid reflux and the intensity of his heartbeat against his neck. He had no guarantees what the Lord would do.

This entire mess was his fault. He should've never agreed to help Derrick in the first place. He told himself he'd said yes to help Derrick out, but when he examined himself, the truth was more complicated. There was an element of pride driving his decisions…a little bit of showing off that he still had what it took to be NSA. He'd wanted to show Derrick that despite "selling out" to the easy life of the corporate world, he still had valuable skills.

He'd been promised no danger. They'd said, "Just help out, and let the guys with guns take over." Instead, the *wrong* guys with guns had taken over and gone after his boys.

And Rachel. The image of her standing between the men and his boys would forever be burned into his memory. His heart slowed ever so slightly. First going after the kidnappers and then standing in the gap…he could never express his feelings of gratitude to her in a real, tangible way. But what was she thinking? She could've been killed.

And that was his fault, too.

Something pressed into his shoulder. He blinked and glanced at the hand patting him.

"James, are you hearing you me?" The streetlights emphasized the whites of Rachel's wide eyes. "Are you okay? You're shaking. You haven't answered a single question."

He returned his focus to the road. He eased up on the gas pedal. Where was he? He took a deep breath. "I'm as okay as a guy can be after seeing gunmen going after his kids and neighbor."

"I get that. Do you need me to drive?"

He recognized an office building up ahead to the right. That meant they were just a few minutes from an on-ramp to the freeway. "No.

I do want to call Derrick, though. And give him a piece of my mind."

"Let me. He's had more than enough time." She reached and took the phone from his hand. Her fingers brushed against his wrist as she did, and his stomach unclenched slightly.

He exhaled. She was right. He needed to get a grip. "The contact is in my phone."

"I figured. You don't want to have it on the car speakers because of the kids, right?"

"I don't want to risk waking them up right now," he acknowledged.

"Understood." The phone lit up the interior of the car, but she turned down the brightness. "Here goes. I'll hand you the Bluetooth when he answers." She held up the phone to her ear.

James held his breath and let the car coast. He heard the tinny ring from where he sat.

"Message." Her voice shook like she was on the verge of crying. She looked to him for what to do.

"Don't leave one," he answered. This was unlike Derrick. Something was keeping Derrick from getting to them. If Derrick couldn't find agents he could trust then what hope did James have? What would they do?

Rachel's head hung low, but she didn't cry, she didn't pepper him with questions.

"How are you handling this so well?" he asked.

She leaned back in the seat, so silent and still he wondered for a second if she'd passed out. "People tell me I'm good in a crisis," she whispered. "I've had plenty of practice."

"You keep mentioning little things about your past that begged to be questioned, but yet you don't want to talk." His tone had bite to it. He recognized the symptoms. If he wasn't careful, he'd end up taking out his frustration on the next person he spoke to. Rachel deserved nothing but kindness, adoration even, from him. "Someday, I hope you can tell me," he said, this time softer. "When you feel comfortable."

"Fair enough," she muttered.

"But answer me this. How'd you know what kind of gun that was?" He turned to her in time to see her roll her eyes.

"Okay. I used to have a mentor—a second mother really—in my life. Meredith knew what I grew up with and helped me escape it. I lost her this year and I suppose all of this—"

She threw up her hands. "I guess part of me really wants to talk about it, and it keeps slipping out, especially with you. Sorry. Bottom line, I grew up with drug dealers. They talked about guns a lot. The SIG-Sauer is the type the Feds use the most. Or used to use. It came to mind in the heat of the moment. I didn't spout it to be accurate, I don't even know if I was.

I just wanted them to believe I knew my way around a gun."

"And do you?"

"Not at all." She shook her head and a tapping sound reached his ears.

He turned and realized her teeth were chattering. Maybe she was just now realizing how close she'd come to getting shot. He reached for her hand and squeezed it. "Where'd you put the gun?"

"It's in my purse."

They drove in silence on the freeway, underneath a couple of exit signs.

"James, where are we going?"

"I wanted to get as much space between us and those guys as possible. I didn't know at first, but now I'm thinking we head directly for Derrick's house. If he hasn't found us a safe house by now then he can take us in himself."

"You know where he lives?"

He nodded. "When Nikki and I used to work for him, we became close. When we left DC and moved here, we kept in touch with Christmas cards and the like… Well, Nikki did at least. She became close friends with his wife, Cynthia. So when Derrick got assigned to run an office here, they invited us over for dinner. I don't know the exact street number, but when I see it, I'll know."

"James?" In the darkness, her voice sounded so soft, so soothing and so vulnerable.

"Yes?"

"When you tied up those men... Did you think to check them for any identification?"

He nodded. "They were clean. No wallet. No NSA badges or driver's licenses. I imagine they kept it in their car. I probably should've checked the sedan, as well, but I didn't think of it."

"How'd they find us?"

The question served as bolt of lightning, jump-starting his brain. He'd been operating on pure emotion and instinct. Rare for him, but so was having his children hunted by gunmen. How *did* they find them? The black sedans he'd seen on the freeway... He'd lost them. Or had they let him think that so they could take him by surprise?

He replayed driving through the subdivision and into the church parking lot. No, they hadn't been following him. He'd been alert and watching. They wouldn't have let them wait that long before going after them, either, if they were that close. Would they?

His dashboard glowed with LCD numbers. The display switched between the temperature and the compass, telling him they were heading due north. He'd told himself those men couldn't possibly be real NSA agents. They were crooks with a leak, able to hear NSA whisperings but not really with the resources the agency could provide. But what if they didn't need NSA resources at all? His breath turned hot.

He didn't want the next exit, but if he had any chance of keeping his children or Rachel safe, they needed to get off as soon as possible. The straight line of the freeway made them easy bait. He flipped on his turn signal and slipped over into the right lane. "Rachel, this is my fault."

"Don't start," she said. "You didn't make those men come after us."

"No, but I sure made it easier."

"What do you mean?"

He glanced sideways at her, wondering if she could handle the truth. He needed her to stay strong and calm. "This is a company car." Saying the words made him furious with himself for not seeing the truth sooner.

He pulled off the freeway but could feel her stare.

"What are you trying to say?"

"It can only mean one thing. We're being tracked."

EIGHT

Rachel pressed her spine into the back of her seat. James didn't decrease his speed as he took the spaghetti-bowl exit. She dug her fingernails into either side of the seat. "I don't see how almost getting us killed will help."

He pressed the brake. "I want to get us somewhere as fast as possible where we can dump the car."

They passed several fast-food joints on the right, but the part of town didn't look familiar. "Do you know where we are?"

"A couple of miles from Derrick's house." He sighed. "I think we need to go by foot." He pointed to a car wash a block up ahead. "I took the boys on a long bike ride on the trails a few weeks back and got turned around up here. Had to look at the map to find my way back. The trail ends at Derrick's subdivision, a few blocks away from his house."

James looked at the rearview mirror. The

traffic had dissipated with the later hour, especially in this part of town. In an uncharacteristic move, he took the turn without signaling. They slipped into a dimly lit stall of the self-serve car wash.

She squinted, trying to see past the rows of bushes beyond the stall. "Are you sure there's a trail back there?"

"Yes. And, hopefully, unless they know this area well, they won't think to pursue us on foot." He cringed and clicked his phone on. "I need to make yet another big ask. I think we need to leave our phones here."

Oh, no. Ask her anything but that. "You think they can track my phone?"

He shrugged. "I don't know, Rachel. I'm trying to eliminate the options." He flipped open his contacts. "I think I've committed to memory all the numbers I'll need."

"My salon," she said. "I have clients coming tomorrow. Saturday is a big day for me."

He nodded. "Can you make a call from here and get some backup before ditching the phone?"

Could she? She considered the salon her baby. She'd built the business from the ground up. Only in the last two years had she bit the bullet and expanded into a new location complete with other stylists. She'd never asked anyone else to step in for her.

Her receptionist, Carly, had just started working for her three months prior and though she peppered Rachel daily with requests for more projects, Rachel had never taken her up on it. It seemed wiser to handle everything but scheduling appointments.

She swallowed and found James staring at her. His knee bounced up and down. "We have to hurry. They could be here any minute."

"But they took a decent amount of time to find us in the church."

He tapped the steering wheel. "I took a convoluted route to get there and we hid the car in a shed that would've diminished the signal. They had a lot to check before breaking into the church. I know I wouldn't have broken in if I weren't sure. So try to make it quick."

"How long do you think it'll be until I can go back to normal?" she asked.

He leaned forward until the top of his forehead rested against the steering wheel. "Two hours ago I'd have said within the day. Now, I don't know. I'm sorry I can't give you any definitive answers."

She pulled up her contact list and pressed Carly's number. As soon as Carly answered, Rachel kept it short and to the point. She asked

Carly to reschedule all of next week's appointments and, aside from asking if everything was okay, Carly surprised her by saying it'd be no problem.

"Okay," James said. "You need to take the battery and the SIM card out of the phone so they can't access any of your contacts. Then I'll snap the SIM cards and throw it all in the trash."

She frowned but removed the backing of her phone "If there is a possibility they're tracking our phones, can't we put the phones on someone else's bumper?"

"It's good thinking, except I don't want these guys targeting innocent bystanders." He turned his own phone over, flicked off the casing and pulled the battery out.

She didn't want anyone in danger, either. Still, it seemed like it'd be a better idea to lead them farther away from their true destination. "Does the river happen to get near the trail?"

His fingers hesitated over the SIM card. A slow grin crossed his features, the light reflecting off his white teeth. "Yes. And we need to go upriver."

"So we float our phones downriver." She unzipped her purse but hesitated to stick her hand inside since the gun still rested in there. If only they had something guaranteed to float. She snapped her fingers. "Snack container."

James hit the latch to the console and it popped open. "Perfect." He removed the rect-angular box and dumped out the raisins into her hands. "It'll be tight if we want the lid on it. We'll have to slip them in diagonally on their side."

She reassembled her phone and placed it inside. "Now let's get it to the river and pray it works."

"Amen," James answered.

His voice sounded so sincere. "Did we just pray?" she asked.

"I find it more efficient to pray than to talk about praying. Let's get moving."

She moved almost on autopilot. The stor-age container didn't fit in her purse next to the gun, but she managed to get it halfway inside. Since she had a gun, she left the bat in the car and threw her backpack on.

The boys didn't blink when she opened the passenger door, even with the interior lights blazing. Caleb seemed twice the weight as she tried to maneuver him into her arms. She'd heard a mother tell her boy not to go "bone-less" on her, and now Rachel understood why. She grunted as she pulled him out of the car and up into her arms.

James managed to carry Ethan, his backpack and Ethan's miniature pack at the same time.

She had to shift Caleb to her hip to do so, but she managed to grab his little bag, too. Caleb made a soft sigh and adjusted, moving his arms around her neck. Her chest expanded with tenderness for the little guy. She'd apparently earned his trust, and it meant the world to her. Or did he have the type of childhood that he trusted all adults? That question would need to be unpacked later.

They met in front of the car. James pointed out a small section between the bushes that they could step past. Moving from the lit city into a dark trail system made her heart jolt.

Safety and control had been her top priorities these last years. As she stepped past the curb into the foliage, it seemed she was leaving her life behind. The gentle breeze brought the scents of bricklebush, sage and primrose.

James took the lead then stopped and held out his left hand while he held Ethan in his right arm. "There's a steep incline here."

Her left arm gripped Caleb tight as she accepted his hand. Their eyes connected, and Rachel's mouth went dry.

"You doing okay?" he asked, his voice gentle.

She blinked. "Yes." He held her hand as he

guided her down the damp grass hill. Given the lack of rain in California she assumed the sprinklers had been run recently. She felt the bumpy pavement underneath the thin soles of her canvas shoes. His fingers slipped from her palm, and an involuntary shiver ran up her spine.

The sound of rushing water complimented the jostling leaves and tree branches above. "We're close."

He pointed. "There's a small slope to the water."

"Can you hold Caleb for a moment?"

He nodded. "You sure you don't want me to do it?"

"I've got it."

He took Caleb into his left arm with ease. Seeing him hold the boys in either arm reminded her of the moment he'd grabbed them from the white van. Had it really been a few hours ago? It seemed like days. The incline to the water wasn't steep, but her eyes strained to see beyond the shadows the trees and bushes created.

The hill bottomed out and her shoes stuck slightly in the dirt. The clouds moved and the moon illuminated the rippling water. Her skin tingled with heightened sensitivity. Every insect and bird call set her on edge. Even though James stood right above the slope, she couldn't see him.

Her fingers wrapped around the container. She bent down to steady the box. Her muscles refused to move faster, even though she should've been done by now. She shivered. Being alone, exposed in the night, her eyes wouldn't stop darting around the area, searching, looking for danger.

The cool water sloshed onto her fingertips. *Please help this go far and lead them away from us.* She lifted her fingers and watched the box rock back and forth before it got pulled into the current.

The mother of Moses set her baby in a basket down the river in hopes he'd float to safety. Did she watch the basket float down the river, praying? Rachel had only known Caleb and Ethan a short while, but she cared enough for them that she couldn't imagine doing the same thing, trusting God enough. Maybe that proved once again she didn't have what it took to be a mom.

The box slipped through the reflection of the moon and then disappeared from her view.

"Rachel." His urgent whisper cut through the sounds of nature. Her shoulders jerked back, and she sprinted up the hill to James.

* * *

His biceps and back already felt the weight of the two children, but he pushed the discomfort from his mind.

Rachel crested the hill. "Is everything okay?" she whispered, looking over his shoulder.

"I heard a car door up there. We need to move." He glanced at her hands. "Did it work?"

"The box is floating."

Finally something went right. He set off on a fast-paced stride into the darkness. If the phone idea worked, they'd be free to approach Derrick's house safely once they rounded the bend and were out of sight.

Rachel shuffled to meet his pace. "Do you want me to take Caleb?" she whispered.

He shook his head. Any change in motion would slow them down, and he really didn't want to see who was behind the car-door noise. The crackling of branches up ahead from the breeze set his teeth on edge. He couldn't pinpoint the source of each noise.

Rachel pumped her arms like a power walker. In any other circumstances he'd find it cute. She looked over her shoulder. Her eyes widened. She grabbed a fistful of his sleeve and yanked him toward her with her other finger on her mouth.

James fought the need to look, but she'd seen something so he couldn't chance extra movements. He darted behind a Douglas fir. Shuffling and slapping feet grew closer. *Please let it be a late-night jogger.* Of course it'd be unwise for anyone to run alone at night on these trails, but it'd be better for them.

Rachel took a step farther into the trees. Either she wanted to feel more hidden, or she was trying to see who was making the noise on the trail. When she shifted, she brushed up against an evergreen branch. It jostled the other branches. One slid across Caleb's arm. He let out an aggravated soft cry.

James stiffened as Caleb shifted and fell back asleep. Rachel spun around, her hand placed over her mouth.

"You hear that?" A man's voice filtered through the trees.

James still had a gun in the back of his jeans. Like Rachel, he'd never used one. He'd participated in paintball wars and nail-gun shooting competitions with his brothers, though. Never before had a weapon been so close to his children. If he were going to reach for it, he'd need to give one of the boys to Rachel, but moving them could cause another outburst.

"Could've been one of those northern mockingbirds."

"No, those things remind me of a cheap alarm clock."

"Shh. They're on the move. Come on, before the signal gets weak again."

So when James noticed his cell reception had dropped to one bar in the church, had their tracking signal suffered? Did that mean they weren't tracking the car, and he could go back to the vehicle? Of course, the car had been in an aluminum shed, which would've also decreased reception. He grunted. The risk wouldn't be worth it. For now, they needed to focus on their new destination.

He counted silently to one hundred, giving the men enough time to be out of earshot before moving back to the path. Rachel reached for him and shook her head. The moon filtered through the woods around them and shined on her royal blue eyes.

She tiptoed away from him, away from the path, and disappeared into the darkness. He pursed his lips. Even if he'd wanted to object, he couldn't. What was she doing? Following the men? He debated following her, but taking the boys deeper into the trees was asking for a branch to the face. He turned to find her in front of him. He inhaled a sharp breath and clenched his jaw to hold in an exclamation. His heart raced. She must have gone clear around the tree.

She put a hand on her mouth and cringed in

silent apology before she beckoned him to follow her with the other hand. His biceps and lower back weren't going to stay silent much longer, though. The strain of carrying two sleeping boys was easier to handle while in motion.

Rachel reached for Ethan and this time, he allowed her to take him. Thankfully, Ethan switched over to her without so much as a sigh. Ethan even snuggled into the small of her neck. His heart twisted at the sight.

James pulled back his shoulders, readjusted Caleb to distribute the weight more evenly, and took a tentative step toward the trail. He peeked around the pointy dark ends of the tree. Not so much as a shadow appeared on the path.

To stay on the safe side, they stuck to the right edge of the trail in a single-file line. It meant less shadows and an easier path into hiding if necessary. After a block worth of speed-walking, the trail bent farther away from the river. He slowed his pace ever so slightly and stepped to the side to walk with Rachel instead of in front of her.

Neither of them said a word, but the sounds of birds and crickets were surprisingly loud. He never thought of the trails as loud before, but as his senses were on high alert it made it hard to hear if someone was coming behind them. His eyes constantly assessed the dark shadows on either side. Every ten steps or so, Rachel looked over her shoulder.

"I think we're out of earshot," he said softly. "But it's in our best interest to keep moving fast. I have no idea how long it'll take them to figure out we duped them. If I knew the speed of the river that'd be another thing," he mumbled. He offered her a small smile. "Your idea to float the phones down the river was the stuff of genius."

She glanced at him. "I thought you didn't like that word, and please don't compare my sorry intellect with yours. You'd have thought of it in another minute."

He gestured with his chin at the fork. "It bought us enough time to get out of sight. I'll feel better when we get to where the trail splits. We'll take the left one and get off as soon as we get close to Derrick's subdivision."

"What if they're waiting for us there?"

He'd considered it, but every muscle hurt, his stomach ached with hunger—a few mini calzones hardly made a dent—and he desperately needed to shut his brain off for a while. "I got nothing. We walk to a hotel? I have some cash, not a ton, but it should cover one night."

"Okay. At least we have a plan. I just feel like I'm missing something."

He slowed his stride. "Why? You had nothing to do with this. Or did you have more questions?"

"No. I mean I'm searching for what we should do next, you know? Like that saying… God helps those who help themselves."

He shook his head. "I've never been a fan of that one. I struggle enough with control issues. If I thought I needed to constantly take matters into my own hands, I'd never be able to sleep."

She shrugged. "I'm not saying I don't have my own control issues, but the principle has gotten me this far."

"Hard work, wisdom and God's grace has brought you success, Rachel."

"Fair enough," she said softly. "Maybe a better saying would be 'God helps those who turn to Him.'"

He smiled. How'd she do it? She made it impossible for him to stop *feeling*. His eyes burned with held-back emotion. "I like that," he finally said. "The split is up ahead."

NINE

Rachel longed to set down Ethan for a minute. The muscles between her shoulder blades screamed as if the tiny muscle fibers were ripping apart. James didn't complain. He hid his strength well.

Until the past twenty-four hours she never knew about his martial arts history or just how fit he kept himself. Modesty in a man seemed like an oxymoron in her past. The men she usually dated didn't waste any time before telling her about how often they worked out.

She glanced at his profile. Just how smart was he if the NSA asked *him* for help? How could she possibly feel like an equal to a genius like him?

The sounds of nature and the darkness kicked her mind into high gear, processing so much of what had just happened. Except the first thing her brain wanted to focus on wasn't the danger but the fact James didn't seem jealous at all when he talked about her date back at the church. Her neck grew hot at the thought even though the breeze should've chilled her.

Why had she insisted they still car-pool? Was she pushing herself on him? Maybe he didn't care one way or the other if they spent any time together. She pursed her lips. If they ever got out of this situation, she couldn't really blame him, and that bothered her even more.

Her blood sugar was probably just low. After eating, her emotions would go back to being even keel, and she wouldn't care so much what her handsome neighbor thought about her.

"We're turning off onto the left path now," he whispered. "Stay close."

Her lower back and hamstrings joined in the complaining as they climbed a hill. They crested the top, and he stopped abruptly. "Uh-oh."

"Oh, no, don't say that," she said. "What? What is it?"

"I don't remember this extra split. I'm not sure which way I'm supposed to turn."

He stepped slowly in a circle, but darkened trees surrounded them except for the long flat thing. Could she sit on it? Upon closer inspection, she confirmed it was a bench, a glorious, wonderful bench. She sat and groaned with relief as her lap took most of Ethan's weight.

James looked down at her. "You know we can't stay here. They're probably already searching the trails for us."

"Just a minute," she pleaded. "I don't know how you're carrying so much. I'm dying."

He joined her on the bench. "Give me Ethan. We have to keep going."

She cringed. She wanted to help and instead she was only slowing them down. "No, no. I'll be fine. Let's go." Her spine screamed at her as she straightened. The moment she started walking, all her muscles burned as if they'd never had a rest in the first place. "I'm sorry," she said.

"Don't be sorry. You cut hair all day. I'm sure your back takes a beating all week. I think we should take a right." His voice was soft and breathy, slightly above a whisper.

"You're sure?"

"Eighty percent…no, ninety percent sure it's the right way." He swung his right foot and kicked at some invisible rock. "I've about had it. I need something to go right."

"Your boys are here with you. I'd call that a pretty big right."

He dropped his head over Caleb. "Thank you. I needed that reminder."

She sighed. She'd give anything for a nice

cold water bottle. The river's background noise heightened her thirst.

"We need to pick up the pace." The sound of their panting seemed to echo in the quiet forest. "I forgot to ask." His voice was soft, hushed. "Is everything going to be okay at your salon?"

"Yes. I've never missed a day there, though."

"What drew you to styling hair?" He glanced down at her, his pace never slowing. "Trust me, thinking about something else will help."

She blinked. "I wanted to help women with inner beauty feel the same way on the outside." The darkness seemed to swallow her whispers. "Most days I wonder if I do it because I want to earn that inner beauty myself." Her mouth dropped. She'd said too much. Thankfully he couldn't see the humiliation on her face.

James didn't even react. He just nodded and kept walking. "Your actions show you have an abundance of it."

She remained speechless. Men only commented on her hair or eyes or physical appearance. No one had ever, except for Meredith, told her she had inner beauty.

"Half a mile left to go. Wanna tell me about your childhood now?"

She scoffed, careful not to laugh aloud. "You're trying really hard to keep my mind off my screaming muscles, aren't you?"

"Busted." He raised an eyebrow but kept his gaze on the trail with frequent glances over his shoulder. "Is it working? Otherwise, let me take Ethan."

Had any other person asked about her childhood, she'd have objected. But James had been right earlier when he'd said she kept alluding to it in front of him. She hadn't known just how desperate she'd been to talk to someone lately, to have someone really know her. "Long story short, it wasn't the nicest area to live. I already told you my parents were drug dealers. So Meredith, the mentor I mentioned, provided students with tutors, and if they kept their grades up, her organization put money in savings for them to get a used car by graduation. When my parents went to jail, Meredith took me in. She passed away this year."

He frowned. "How?"

"Old age. She was a spunky lady full of life. Sassy, too."

"Ah, so that's where you get it."

She smirked. "I got my determination from her. She changed my life. She built me up, showed me I had value and helped me get the skills needed to run my own business."

"God sets the lonely in families. It's in Psalms."

Her cheeks heated. Was he trying to imply she needed a new family now?

"I didn't mean…I—I wasn't…." He stammered, as if reading her mind. He turned suddenly. "Seriously, give me Ethan. I thought I heard something."

Fear outranked pride. She shoved the boy into his arms and he took off. She could barely keep up with his run. The moment they rounded a corner he slowed and darted into the trees. The moonlight combined with the streetlights flickering past a set of evergreen trees helped her to see him better.

Rachel followed him over the branches littering the ground. He took slow steps. Her ears strained to pinpoint the sound of shuffling. She wanted to whisper, to alert James, but he stepped behind an evergreen tree and froze.

Their eyes met, and she stepped closer to him, covered by shadows. The shuffling grew louder and while Rachel could hold her breath there was no way to stop the boys' steady breathing. The shuffling slowed.

Her throat closed. She couldn't cower in fear and wait for him to discover them. One more sound out of the boys and they'd be found for sure.

Rachel bent down slowly, ignoring James's wide eyes. She tentatively spread out her fingers onto the ground, praying she didn't touch a snake or spider. Her fingertips brushed up against a rock. She slid her palm over the top, gripped it and popped it out of the mud. In one fluid motion, she stood, pulled back her arm and threw it as hard as she could. *Please let it fly far away.*

A satisfying thud and crackle sounded down the hill followed by flapping wings. The shuffling pants moved. Then stopped again. A light beam shone down the path they'd just come from. She heard James release a small gasp. What had she done? If the beam found them...

"Hey," a deep voice called. The beam hit two men on bicycles. "Sir. You can't be here. It's after dark. The trails are closed."

The beam shut off. "Uh, o-okay," the man stammered. "I'll just go back to my car."

"Sir, would you like an escort?"

"That's not necessary," the man retorted.

Rachel recognized that voice without seeing him. The man was the same one that had pointed the gun at them in the garage and shot at the car. She shivered.

The officers waited on the bicycles until the man passed them before turning their bikes around. Rachel exhaled, her insides shaking. James's warmth left her as he trekked deeper into the woods.

They stepped between two giant evergreens and onto a suburban sidewalk. "We're exposed."

While very few streetlights lit the neighborhood, light fixtures decorated every garage. She wanted to dart back into the woods.

"That was too close," James said.

Obviously he realized his momentary lapse of judgment when he'd called her genius earlier. "It was foolish," she said. "I just didn't want him to discover us."

James didn't agree, but he also didn't argue. Her cheeks heated at her mistake, probably a mistake a parent never would've made.

He nodded toward the houses. "I'm hoping we look like a family on a late-night walk, trying to get our little ones asleep. But we need to get out of sight fast."

A block down the sidewalk, he stepped into the shadows underneath a tree.

She peeked around his shoulder. "Are we stopping?"

"There's a black sedan parked on the road up ahead. I can't be sure but I thought I saw a flicker of light inside the car."

"Is it the same men?" She squinted to look for herself.

"Impossible. They were on the trail just a few moments ago. It'll take them a while to get back to their vehicle." He sighed. "It's probably nothing…residents with too many cars for the garage or guests, but to be on the safe side we need to go through the community area."

"Those are closed after nightfall," she commented. "We'll be going between everyone's backyards."

"Then we better move quickly." He set off through the tiny space between two backyards until he reached the path. The majority of the subdivisions in the area had community areas between the rows of cookie-cutter houses to help appease homeowners over the fact their backyards were the size of small garages. The area was not lit up by lights, though, hence the rule about being closed after dark. The moon, now hidden by clouds, provided barely enough light to keep from running into each other.

"How will you know which house is Derrick's from the back?"

"Because it's at the end of the row." He lengthened his stride so much she almost jogged to keep up. They reached it in record time.

"I need a free arm." He slipped Caleb into her arms. "Stay here for a second, okay?"

He stepped away before she could refuse. She shivered in the dark and looked over her shoulder to make sure she was alone. Shapes that could be men, but were probably trees and bushes, lined the area. She leaned her back against the fence for support.

If it weren't for Caleb's warm body, she'd be cold. She bent down, and her cheek brushed against his forehead. He remained warm in her arms. His long eyelashes spilled over onto his chubby cheeks, completely in a state of peaceful rest.

She could see the appeal in motherhood. The thought jolted her. James approached. "This is definitely the house. There is a guy sitting in a sedan out front."

"With the car running?" she asked.

He sighed. "No. Lights off. That's what worries me."

"He didn't see you, did he?" Panic closed her throat. If she had to run any more she wouldn't be able to hold one of the boys. Her arms, back and legs were about to give. "What are we going to do?"

"We go in the backyard and hope Derrick can help us out. It's all I've got." He reached over her head and flicked a metal latch.

She stepped backward as the cedar door swung forward. A citrus smell wafted past, both invigorating and appetizing. The moon and their wide eyes reflected off the glass back door covered by vertical blinds.

James raised a fist. "Let's hope we don't

scare them to death." He knocked three times, lightly, on the metal frame surrounding the glass. A minute passed by as they stood shoulder to shoulder waiting.

"Maybe they're not home?"

A bright light flooded the back patio. "Duck," James said.

She squatted and turned her head away, shoving her eyes closed until the throbbing passed. She blinked as Caleb squirmed in her arms, fully awake, and unhappy. In the corner of the yard, a short lemon tree proved the source of the smell.

"Stay down," James instructed. "In case anyone sees our heads poking over the fence. Boys, I need you to be quiet for just a moment."

"Where are we, Daddy?" Caleb asked.

The blinds shifted and a petite blonde woman with a stomach the size of two beach balls stood behind the door, pushing aside a space between the hanging blinds. She held something metallic at the side of her hip. A gun? The woman squinted at James before her eyes widened in recognition.

James placed a finger on his mouth, silently begging her to be quiet. She frowned but opened the door and gestured them forward. "James?" she whispered. "What's going on?"

They stepped into the tiled dining area, and

James flipped the switch to turn the backyard light off. "I'm sorry to barge in so late, Cynthia. I need to talk to Derrick right away."

She smiled at the boys, but her forehead remained creased in a frown. "He left over two hours ago to meet you. I tried him a few minutes ago. He isn't answering his phone."

James closed his eyes. Derrick would've answered his phone for his very pregnant wife. Last he'd heard, Cynthia was supposed to be on modified bed rest until the twins were due. But he didn't want to worry Cynthia more than usual. "I'm sure we got our wires crossed."

She glanced at him with a smile, but it didn't meet her eyes. "No need to tiptoe around the truth, James. I'll try him again."

"Don't leave a—"

"A message," she finished for him. She held up a hand. "I don't know what's going on, and I don't want to know. But this isn't my first rodeo." Cynthia stepped into the kitchen and placed the gun she'd been attempting to hide on top of the refrigerator. She lifted a wicker basket filled with bananas and presented it to the twins. "You boys look hungry."

Caleb and Ethan both wore huge grins that spoke of their affection for Cynthia, but they kept their chins tucked to their chests, a sign they were feeling shy.

"You've got a man outside, Cynthia."

Her face paled. "He's still there? He showed up shortly after Derrick left." She sighed. "It's why I tried to call him a while ago to see if he'd ordered a detail. He always tells me first." She patted her stomach. "Let me make sure all the blinds are closed. We've already installed light-blocking shades in preparation for the babies. Stay here a minute."

He smiled in response. Cynthia and Derrick had been trying to have kids ever since he'd met them years ago, fresh out of high school. He'd never seen Derrick so happy when he'd announced they were expecting twins.

Derrick was supposed to have been here or at least have been available by phone. James never would've come if he had thought his presence would put Cynthia into danger.

Cynthia returned. "Okay. Our *friend* outside shouldn't be able to see anything now." She picked up her cell phone and hit a button. She held it to her ear. "I'm Cynthia," she said, looking past him.

James spun around. "Oh, I'm sorry. This is Rachel, my neighbor. I—" He started to explain, but stopped short. "You don't want to know."

"Well, it's nice to meet you, Rachel. Any friend of James…" Cynthia frowned. "Voice mail." She clicked it off, sighed and placed a hand underneath her very large, oblong stomach. "Can I assume that since you came in through my back door, you don't have a car?"

He nodded.

"Would I be correct in deducing you have nowhere else to go?"

"You'd be a regular Sherlock," Rachel said.

Cynthia looked at the ceiling. "I can't reach Derrick. So I'm thinking you guys should stay here until I do. It's late, so if you want to put the boys down, use Derrick's office. It has a futon and no windows."

James pressed a hand against his forehead. Nothing was going right. "Cynthia, you're supposed to be on bed rest, right?"

She raised an eyebrow. "Modified. I'm allowed to move around the house as long as I take it easy."

James studied the boys, who were almost done with their bananas. Unless they heard a kitten meow or a dog bark, they would fall back to sleep quickly. He didn't think they'd try to look out the windows, especially at night.

"Okay, I'll take you up on it. But tell me what to do. You rest."

Cynthia acquiesced and took her place at a recliner near the door, a gun back in her possession, hidden by a quilted throw she draped over her lap.

Rachel grabbed some pillows from the linen closet in the hallway. They each took an end of the fitted mattress sheet meant for the futon in the study and made short work of preparing the boys' bed. "Do you think the man outside is from the NSA?" she asked.

The boys seemed engaged with the TV show playing softly in the opposite corner. "I don't know," James answered. "Didn't it strike you as odd that the guy following us in the woods didn't tell the officers he was NSA?"

She shrugged. "Maybe only one of them has an NSA badge." Her eyes widened. "Worse case scenario, could they be listening or checking heat sensors on this place right now?"

On any other day, the very idea would've made him laugh. How sad that the thought had crossed his mind, as well. "That's what I had to check before we came inside. No, there's no surveillance vans close enough to do what you're asking." James looked at his boys. "But I have no guarantee how long we can stay here," he whispered. "Derrick is still our best shot, but if he's not in contact by morning, we need to leave anyway."

"How?"

His head ached at the very thought. "I haven't figured that out yet."

A yawn ripped past her throat which triggered a yawn of his own. In the dimly lit room such a simple act seemed intimate.

It was ridiculous, but after his thoughtless comment about God putting the lonely in families, he felt awkward around her. He'd meant that God had taken care of her by giving her Meredith, but it hadn't come out that way. And she no longer had Meredith, so it must've sounded like he was throwing her pain back in her face, which was the last thing he'd wanted to do.

He stared at the plush carpet and ached to kick off his shoes and stretch out. If only he could close his eyes and forget the last twenty-four hours. He'd wake up to find everything sorted out. Derrick would be back and tell him the danger had passed, that he hadn't risked his cushy job that enabled him to pay the bills and work from home a bulk of the time. If only.

The smell of Rachel's hair brought him back to the real world. If Derrick took much longer, he'd be taking the floor beside his boys tonight. But, with a strange man sitting outside the house, he took the responsibility of protecting Cynthia, Rachel and his boys very seriously.

There would be no sleep tonight.

TEN

Rachel rolled over on the twin bed and stared at the two cribs on the opposite wall. Cynthia had insisted she take a rest while they wait for Derrick. "I'm sure he's just swamped sorting things out," she'd said, but her eyes had lacked luster, worry lines creasing her forehead.

Judging by how tense James had seemed, she didn't think he was entirely sold on the idea, either. Yet, it was probably the best scenario for the boys. Why'd it have to be a nursery? She'd never once questioned her decision to avoid motherhood at all costs until now.

Her heavy eyes closed as she tried to take deep breaths, but the only picture in her mind was a car sitting outside. She flinched and looked at the blue LED clock on the bottom shelf of the diaper station. She'd apparently fallen asleep for forty-five minutes out of pure exhaustion, but dreams of trying to keep men from Caleb and Ethan woke her up, covered in a cold sweat.

Everything hurt. Rachel took deep breaths. *God sets the lonely in families.* She longed to have her phone to look up the passage in the Bible. James said it was in Psalms somewhere.

Cynthia seemed like she would make a good mother. She'd told James her parents and Derrick's parents would alternate staying at their house for a few weeks once their twins were born. She probably had examples of nurturing, good parents in abundance.

It was true God had given her Meredith when she'd needed it most. One of her coworkers always talked about friends like they were family. Maybe that's what she needed, to open herself up more to friends and to learn about what it was to be a family that way.

The blinds tempted her. A peek would ease her mind whether the man in the mysterious vehicle still sat outside the house. She restrained herself. If he was out there and saw movement, he might get curious. And what if the black sedan had joined them? At least they had taken their guns away. Though, with men like that, guns might be a dime a dozen.

She rolled over. The night-light shone on the ceiling's grooves. James had looked so strong and handsome in the moonlight. Thoughts like those would not help her get back to sleep. She'd never realized how tethered she was to her smartphone until now without a game to play or a book to read.

Rachel sat up, fully awake. Her hair, slightly damp from a late-night shower, fell onto her shoulders. She stood and tugged her T-shirt down to cover the back of her sweatpants. She twisted the doorknob softly and tested the wooden floor for creaks. The last thing she wanted was to wake anyone after such a physically and emotionally exhausting day.

She tiptoed to the kitchen where she found the oven hood light still on. A Sudoku book had been on the coffee table so if she found a pen, she'd be set. On the countertop, next to the refrigerator, a stack of bills was in a cute, wicker basket along with…yes, pens. She grabbed a blue one and turned around right into James.

She gasped and a tiny squeak escaped her lips. "You scared me." The whisper came out more like a hiss.

"I could say the same for you."

"Did I wake you?"

His blue eyes were alert. The only sign of exhaustion was the lack of a smile. His dark brown hair begged to be styled. She could do so much with it. He wore a plain gray T-shirt and black sweatpants.

"I'm not convinced it's safe to sleep yet," he admitted. He held his right arm strangely.

She tilted her head. A gun was in his hand, pointed to the ground. She no longer felt chilly. "I'm glad you didn't lead with that."

He nodded. "Never. But why didn't you come out here with yours?"

"First, it's not mine and never will be. And, I guess I didn't think about it. The doors are locked, and Cynthia put a gun on top of the fridge."

"No, she took hers to bed. Besides, locks aren't going to stop those men if they think we're in here."

She remembered the sound of glass breaking all too well. She crossed past him into the living room and settled on the suede couch, picking up the Sudoku book. He followed her into the room. "You don't think Cynthia would mind if I did one of the puzzles to calm my brain, do you? I could pay her back."

"If it's out here, Cynthia would want guests to use it. She's the queen of hospitality." He placed the gun on the coffee table and sat on the opposite end of the couch, moving the throw pillow to behind his back.

"Maybe you should sleep out here on the couch instead of the floor."

He shook his head. "It wouldn't matter. Floor is probably better for my back anyway."

"I could take the Sudoku back to the nursery if I'm keeping you awake."

"I'd rather you do it here." He pointed to the curtains. "I haven't checked the nursery, but this room has both blinds and blackout curtains. The oven light from the kitchen is on. I'm sorry, but I'm afraid I don't feel comfortable adding any other light."

She flipped open the book. If she squinted she could see clear enough.

"We both work when we're overwhelmed." He smiled that same crooked smile that seemed to say *I know you.*

"It probably seems silly to you—a hairdresser who hates math but loves Sudoku. You could probably do these in your sleep."

"Not at all. Games like that stimulate my mind. I can use the LINQ query to figure—"

"The what?"

"In simplest terms, it's a computer programming language, but I understand the appeal of Sudoku. For people who are better at other things, they find it relaxing."

"Exactly." Rachel flipped to a puzzle labeled Easy. "It keeps me from thinking about people and my feelings. It tricks my mind into believing I have control, even though I know only God does." She tapped the pen on the page. "If life is crazy and I'm having a hard time letting go, I can at least make this box neat and orderly."

It might not work with a handsome neighbor sitting next to her, though. In her peripheral, she could see him studying her. It made it hard to focus on the numbers and empty blocks. They all seemed a blur, and her mind wouldn't process.

He leaned toward her, his breath hot on her cheek as he pointed at one. "Nine."

Her cheeks heated. "Thanks."

"Do you mind if I give you a tip?"

"Um, okay." If he started trying to teach her the LINQ query, though, she was going to leave.

"I noticed when you punched that man in your house your form was slightly off."

She set down the book in her lap, surprised at the sudden turn of conversation. "How?"

"You had good power from your core. You took martial arts at one time?"

"No. Lots of self-defense classes, though."

"That explains the quick-thinking. Good job using the rolling pin, by the way." He held his arm straight out. "Your fist was also tight, but your knuckles went head-on into him. It got the job done, but if he were any thicker, it would've hurt you." He adjusted his wrist slightly. "Now look. Notice how the back of my fist resembles more of a diamond shape. The goal being that the line of my radius and the first knuckle make a straight line."

Rachel leaned over until she could stare down his arm. "Huh. And that makes a difference?"

He stood and picked up a throw cushion. "You'll try it and always remember. Come on," he whispered. "We can't sleep anyway."

She blinked. He was serious. She set the book aside and stood. "Won't we wake people up?"

"Not unless you knock me over."

The taunt heated her core. "How long were you in martial arts?"

He shrugged. "A long time. Black belt in Tang Soo Do and jujitsu. Doesn't do much good if someone points a gun at you, though." His chin dropped. "You could've been killed at the church."

"But you stopped them."

He shook his head. "I don't take the credit for that. By God's grace, whatever you sprayed in that man's eyes stunned him. But it could've gone so wrong, Rachel." His voice turned gravelly, and his face contorted as if in pain. He rolled back his shoulders and cupped the throw pillow with his right hand. He moved the target to the center of his chest. "Now punch this like you did the man in your house."

She raised an eyebrow. "You realize you sound like one of those guys challenging a girl to punch him as hard as they can, right?"

"No, there's a big difference. I know how to take a punch."

She shrugged, adjusted her stance and punched.

She watched his face, studying him for any signs of pain. His mouth spread into a slow grin. "I'm fine, but I want you to pay attention to how it felt. Did you feel the force of the punch vibrate up your arm?"

"Yes." Add it to the list of discomfort her poor bones and muscles were recovering from.

"That's what I thought. Now look at your wrist and the top of your hand. Try it the way I explained. Lead with those two knuckles and hit me again."

The fist came at him so fast he almost didn't have time to shift his stance.

She grinned. "That's a huge difference. I hardly felt a thing."

"Felt more powerful, too. Want to try one more time?"

She looked into his eyes, and he held her gaze. His mouth went dry.

She adjusted her stance and threw another punch.

He caught it with the pillow. "Good." He used his left hand to touch the outside of her arm. "Don't lock your elbow, though. And if you twist your hips as you punch, you'll have more power."

She nodded but said nothing. Her skin felt on fire underneath his fingers.

"I just want to keep you safe," he whispered.

She nodded. "You're doing a good job." Her voice was so soft he barely heard her. They stood inches apart. He realized his hand was still on her arm. She dropped her fist from his chest, and her hair spilled over her shoulder, tickling his forearm.

The throw pillow slipped between them to the ground. He leaned forward at the same time as she did to get it. She placed a hand on his arm, a soft laugh escaping her lips.

She looked at his mouth, and he couldn't help but return the favor. "Rachel..." He reached for her, his hand slipping behind her neck. She released a soft sigh and tilted her chin upward. His lips brushed hers.

She jerked backward, her eyes wide, her

hand against her mouth, shaking her head. "I'm sorry. I can't," she whispered.

His chest burned, his breath suddenly hot and shallow. He should've never… He stared at the wooden floor and simply nodded. He couldn't process, he couldn't think. He grabbed the gun off the coffee table and made his way back to the study. At the corner he turned back. "Rachel, next time bring the gun with you."

She nodded but didn't make eye contact.

What had he done?

The woman had risked everything for his kids, and he'd thanked her by scaring her with a kiss? He'd let himself operate on assumptions, on instinct, imagining she'd wanted to kiss him as much as he'd wanted to kiss her. He should win a trophy for such poor judgment. He slipped back into the study and closed the door most of the way.

The night-light revealed Caleb and Ethan both peacefully asleep on the futon. He'd never been so thankful that his three-year-olds were still good sleepers. They'd done so well when presented with danger. They took their fear to him and trusted him to take care of it.

His neck tingled with conviction. He used to be pretty fearless himself…confident that God would take care of whatever came his way. When he'd met Nikki he'd *known* somehow she liked him. His heart had ripped in two the day she passed.

Maybe it was too much to ask to ever be able to experience even a fraction of that kind of love again. His heart was crippled. How could he expect Rachel to ever be interested in a man like him?

The floorboards creaked outside his room. He peeked out the door and saw her retreating form go back to the nursery. He exhaled. Should he have apologized? If only Derrick would've found them places to go by now. That's how it should've gone. They should've never been placed in this position.

James took a deep breath to calm his racing heart. How quickly he jumped from embarrassment to anger. He lowered himself to the carpet. Setting the gun far enough away he wouldn't accidentally hit it, but making sure it was still in arm's reach, he stretched out.

Help. It was the only prayer he could utter. His mind and emotions were too jumbled. He took a deep breath and listened to the breathing patterns of his twins.

Ding-dong.

James sat upright, his head pounding. The red LCD numbers from the small clock on the bookshelf read 4:07 a.m. James reached for his gun, checked that the boys were still asleep and rushed to the study door.

Rachel stood at the nursery door, her purse hanging diagonally across her body, unzipped. Cynthia stepped into the hallway. "Are you expecting someone?" he asked.

She shook her head. "I'll check the peephole."

James motioned for Rachel to stay back as he followed Cynthia to the front door. The sun had yet to make an appearance for the day. She flipped the switch by the door. Light spilled from the peephole. She rose on her tiptoes, her stomach pressing into the door as she took a look.

Cynthia dropped to her heels and looked at James, her forehead wrinkled. "It's one of Derrick's men," she whispered.

He stood, paralyzed, unsure of what to do. Should she answer or not? Maybe this was the help he was so desperate for. Cynthia waved him back. He retreated to the corner of the hallway where Rachel waited. They were out of sight from the front door but could still see Cynthia unlock the dead bolt.

"Cynthia," a deep voice said. "I'm sorry to tell you this…"

Cynthia gasped and placed a hand on her mouth. "Oh, please, no…"

"He's still alive," the voice continued. "We found him in a ditch early this morning."

Cynthia's crying made it hard to decipher everything the man said. James's gut twisted, remembering when a policeman had knocked on his own door.

"What happened?" she cried. "Is he gonna—"

"It was a hit-and-run. There's a lot of internal bleeding. He's in surgery now. They're doing their best, Cynthia."

"Have they…have they found who did it?"

Judging by the way Cynthia cried, the answer was no. James knew the feeling. He still didn't know who had plowed their vehicle into Nikki's.

Rachel grabbed James's elbow. She looked in shock. James didn't know what to say. He was reeling himself.

"I'm here to take you to the hospital," the man said.

Cynthia stepped backward, wrapping her arms around herself, tears rushing down her cheeks. "Of course. Give me a bit to get myself together, okay?"

"I'll be waiting in my car."

"Thank you." Cynthia closed the door.

James crossed the room in half a second. Cynthia grabbed both of his forearms, squeezing them as her head dropped and she took deep breaths. "I'm so sorry," he said, the words barely making it past his choked throat.

She sniffed and straightened. "Derrick would want us to keep our heads on straight. Right?" She tightened her grip on him but looked at the ceiling. "There's no way that was an accident, was it?"

James didn't know what to say. The timing did make it look suspicious, but he also knew from experience that tragedy like this happened.

Cynthia didn't mind his silence. "If they got Derrick, it's not safe here. The moment I leave with Derrick's man, they might come in here. Get those boys somewhere safe, away from here, away from whoever hurt my Derrick. Okay? You keep those boys safe, James."

He knew by the tone of her voice that she was trying to be encouraging, but it didn't take away the helplessness gnawing at his chest. Where would they go?

Cynthia dropped one hand to her stomach. "He *has* to get better."

James turned to Rachel. "Gather your things."

"But what about the man watching the house?"

"I think I have a way to take care of that," Cynthia answered. "At least, I'm going to try."

James didn't comment as he made his way to wake up the boys. His mind stayed on Derrick, in surgery right now. *Please let him make it, Lord.* His heart couldn't take any more sorrow.

ELEVEN

Rachel's hands shook. The space inside her ribs felt hollow, the same horrible feeling she got whenever she was sleep-deprived.

Cynthia stepped out of her bedroom, her face freshly washed but without a trace of makeup. She wore a maroon maternity blouse, jeans and loafers with a black leather bag in her right hand.

"You packed fast."

"It's my hospital to-go bag. I didn't think I'd need to go to the hospital for this, though." Her voice cracked. Without thinking, Rachel opened her arms, and Cynthia clung to her.

A movement to the side caused them to stand straight. The boys stood in matching blue shirts and blue pants. Their eyelids hung low, but they wore small smiles. "Go to the potty, then we go," James said, bringing up the rear with their backpacks.

Cynthia stepped into the living room and

jotted something on a piece of paper. "Get a burner phone. Go somewhere remote then call me." She handed him the note. "If I see a strange number on my phone and know something new, I'll pick up. If I don't, I'll let it ring. Don't leave a message."

"Understood."

Cynthia walked past the dining area and opened a door Rachel presumed led to the garage. A moment later the garage door motor hummed. Car doors opened and shut.

James mirrored Rachel's confused expression. "What do you think is happening out there?" she asked.

James strode to the door and looked out the peephole. "Cynthia got out the van, and the agent rushed up to meet her. She's waving her hands, upset about something. Oh. Get back. She's coming this way."

They both hustled into the hallway lest someone see them from the outside.

Cynthia stepped into the living room and shut the door behind her. "I was going to point out the man watching the house, but he's gone. I imagine he left when the agent showed up to get me. I started thinking about what Derrick would do, and it gave me an idea." She crossed over to the basket next to the refrigerator and picked up a set of keys. "I want you to take the spare. You're going to take my keys, use my minivan—it's all decked out with a full tank of gas."

"We can't take your van," Rachel said from behind them. "You won't have a way to get back."

Cynthia looked around James. "I'll have my sister meet me at the hospital. She lives in town. I won't want to stay here until Derrick is better, anyway. Besides, I had the car all set up for car seats. Detach the top halves and it works as booster seats for the boys."

James pointed over her shoulder. "What'd you tell the agent?"

"I said I was in no condition to drive. Instead of following me, I asked him to take me instead."

"Isn't he going to be curious why you came back inside?" Rachel asked.

"I told him I had to use the bathroom again." Cynthia rubbed her stomach, which looked larger than the night before to Rachel. "Stay safe." She stepped back outside.

"Where are we going to go?" Rachel asked.

"I think I should get you and the boys as far away from here as possible and wait until the launch is over."

"When will that be?"

"If someone is able to fix my virus? Sunday."

"But you said that'd be impossible."

"No, I don't have super powers." He shrugged. "It'd just be extremely hard."

"And wouldn't that mean they would get away with launching an EMT?"

His mouth moved into a smirk. "You mean EMP, electromagnetic pulse."

"Yeah, that."

"I'll alert the air force or someone will get involved to shoot it down before it detonates. If it launches, then they will have no need to go after my boys. Granted, that would mean I'll need to trust someone other than Derrick, but at least you and the boys will, theoretically, be out of danger by then."

The somberness of the situation settled on her shoulders. "You want to leave right away."

"The sun is going to rise in an hour or two. I think it's the best solution."

"I'll grab my pack." She headed back into the nursery. A thin light from headlights slipped through the space between the light-blocking shade and the wall and then abruptly turned off. Odd.

She stepped to the side of the window and pressed her back against the wall. She held her breath and lifted the shade with her index finger. To the east of the house a car parked, with his lights off. Their "friend" had returned.

"Come on, boys, let's head for the door."

She wanted to holler but instead ran for the hallway. "No, wait." James turned around. The boys already had their backpacks on. She didn't want to frighten them. "I, uh, saw a thing outside. And I'd like to eat breakfast here," she adlibbed. "I think there are more bananas in the kitchen."

Ethan stood on his tiptoes, trying to peek into the kitchen.

James frowned. "Great," he muttered. "I thought we'd have at least five minutes to leave." He spun around in a circle, searching the walls. "And we're completely without a phone. Sometimes I miss the days everyone had house phones."

Rachel racked her brain for ideas of what to do. If they left now, they'd be spotted, but if they sat in the house much longer, with Cynthia gone, they would likely come inside to check things out.

A small light bobbed through the slits on the right side of the kitchen window, the only window without light-blocking shades. She leaned forward and peeked, confident the car on the opposite side of the house wouldn't be able to see her since the window faced the backyard. A jogger with a headlamp ran through the path, past the house.

Rachel gasped. "I have an idea." She ran around the counter, depositing her purse on top. "Watch this for me, James." She unlocked the back door.

"Where are you going?"

"No time. Trust me."

She slipped out the glass door and ran through the short backyard. She left the fence ajar slightly and sprinted down the path. In her hoodie, T-shirt and sweatpants, she hoped she looked like a jogger, but the canvas shoes didn't really fit the profile. In the dark, maybe it wouldn't be noticeable. The cool air chilled her skin.

The jogger slowed to a stop at a bench at the far end of the community area. She pulled her foot backward to stretch her quadriceps but looked at Rachel in alarm. "Excuse me," Rachel called, hoping she didn't scare her away.

The jogger pulled out an ear bud, looking at her suspiciously. She wore reflective running gear and gloves.

"Nice to meet a fellow early morning runner," Rachel said. The jogger nodded slowly but didn't say a word as she switched legs to stretch. "I'm hoping you can do me a favor. I don't have my phone with me, but there's a strange guy in a sedan who has been sitting at the corner watching everyone."

The jogger raised her eyebrows and pointed in the direction of Cynthia's house. "That corner? I live just down the street."

"Yeah, did you notice him there yesterday, too, watching? I mean, one day you think it might be coincidence but two…"

The jogger fumbled with her shirt, which looked to have a zipper along the waist. She pulled out her phone. "I'm calling the police."

Rachel tried not to smile. "Thank you. I hope the rest of your run is good. Stay safe."

The jogger nodded, but she was already talking to the dispatcher as she jogged off.

Rachel turned to run back to Cynthia's house, satisfied the police would come and chase away the guy staking the house out, at least for a little bit. A dark figure stepped out of the shadows and grabbed her arm.

"I thought that was you," the voice growled.

Rachel screamed, hoping the jogger would get her some help. Instead the man twisted Rachel's left arm behind her back until she was in such pain she could barely breathe.

"Not smart." The man's hot breath brushed past her neck.

Rachel knew that voice. The same voice that almost found them in the woods. "Where's your friend?" Rachel asked.

"Oh, don't you worry about that." He chuckled. "He never thought you'd be stupid enough to come here, but I didn't have that much faith in you. Looks like I'm right." He pressed down on her arm again, forcing her to bend over.

One hand left her back but her attacker's other hand still had a firm, painful grip on her left arm. She heard shuffling and then he spoke, probably into a phone. "Yeah, I got the girl. I'm thinking they're in the house. Yeah, tell him for me. I've got my hands full."

James and the boys…they weren't safe. Once again her foolish attempt to help ended in putting them into jeopardy even more. She dropped her head, and her gaze fell on the darkened outline of a thick branch. She lifted her torso slightly, panting against the pain.

Rachel stomped her right foot onto the stick. The opposite end flung up. She grabbed it with her right hand and swung it diagonally across her body and around the back of her head.

The man groaned at the same time his grip loosened on her arm. She twisted into his hold, pulled back her fist and slammed it into his chest. The moment her knuckles made contact, she knew James had been right about technique. The man jerked back, but Rachel didn't wait for his next move.

She sprinted toward Cynthia's house. She had to warn them. She had to get them out.

Crack!

Rachel stumbled. A searing, sharp pain moved through her left shoulder. She cried out and pulled her arm close to her torso. Another gunshot rang through the open air but either Rachel was in too much shock to feel it or the second one didn't make contact. She pressed forward, slammed the fence open and stumbled toward the glass door.

The past five minutes seemed to last an hour. He'd found some cereal in the pantry so the boys were still occupied as he stared out into the dark backyard. Where was she?

His gut still churned from the horror of finding out Derrick had been hurt. The possibility of Derrick's children having to grow up without having known him was too horrible to ponder. And he couldn't think about Cynthia because he knew how it felt raising two children without the other parent. He'd never wish it on anyone, even if it meant they'd be able to understand the constant battle of trying to make up for the missing parent, trying to be perfect to the point of exhaustion.

A shadow moved. He could barely make out the back fence moving. He saw the telltale sway of long hair in a ponytail and knew it had to be Rachel. James opened the glass door. His hand shook as he flipped the latch to lock it behind her. "What'd you just do? If you were gone another minute, I was coming after you."

She shivered and her right hand pressed into the outside of her left. "Later. Leave. Leave now." Her face tight with pain, she whispered, "They're coming."

"Okay I'll grab the packs and—"

She was shaking her head violently.

"Are you okay?"

"No time."

The tone of her voice left no room for argument. Wordlessly, he grabbed the boys and barreled to the front door. They whimpered, but the early morning exhaustion kept their cries from growing into tantrums.

He looked over his shoulder to see Rachel, her hand bright red, reaching for her purse as she made her way toward him. "Rachel?

Her face paled as she waved her right hand to keep moving. What had happened? The confusion and desperation of the moment made it hard to concentrate without answers. His pulse pounded in his neck and fingertips.

He inhaled and flung the front door open. A police officer approached the driver of the sedan. The cruiser was parked behind him. Approaching sirens could be heard. The officer reached over to hit the radio on his shoulder.

Whatever was going on, James's gut told him to move fast.

Rachel slipped into the passenger side of the minivan in a heartbeat. James deposited the boys in the side door. He ripped off the backs of the car seats like Cynthia had described and flung them into the far back. "I need you to show me how you buckle yourselves, boys." He hopped in the driver's side and backed out of the driveway in three seconds flat.

"I did it, Daddy," Ethan called. "I didn't need Caleb's help this time. I did it by self."

"Good job, buddy," James replied. He kept his eyes on the mirrors. It was still dark enough for headlights, but he debated turning them off. In the end, without proof of ownership, he decided to be a law-abiding citizen. "Wanna tell me what happened out there? More specifically, what happened to your shoulder? Are you even okay?"

Rachel nodded and tilted her head to the boys. "Guys. See the headphones in those pockets? If you put them on you can hear the music." She jutted her chin to the radio. "Look. Press that button and they can listen to something while we talk."

He didn't exactly have time to browse the radio stations. So far the cop and the sedan hadn't pursued him, but without knowing what had happened to Rachel, he had no idea what to expect. He pressed one of the presets, confident Cynthia wouldn't have chosen anything inappropriate. The boys didn't seem to mind, whatever it was.

Rachel licked her lips. "I asked a fellow morning runner to get the police to check out the corner. That way our *friend* would still have no idea we were ever here. And at first it worked. That's why the officer was keeping him busy. Except, the other sirens you hear... they're coming because one of the men following us, he—he grabbed me. Said that someone else was on his way to get you. I got away but not before he shot me."

His muscles jolted as if shocked. "He what?" It was all James could do to keep both hands on the steering wheel. "We have to take you to the hospital now."

"No," she cried. "Get us out of town. Please. I...I think it's just a graze, anyway."

Two police cars zoomed past them, sirens wailing, headed the opposite way. An ambulance brought up the tail. It was tempting to turn the van around and follow them.

"How do you know it's just a graze? Have you even taken a good look?"

"No, but keeping pressure on it is all I can do for now anyway. The point is that man has no problem shooting at us. I don't think he cares so much if any of us make it alive. He didn't seem to worry about leverage with me."

A wave of nausea rushed over him. "They've grown impatient."

"Desperate," Rachel added. "At least this man was. Go back to your plan where you get us far away from them. We need to be hidden."

The thought of Rachel being shot…of his own kids possibly facing bullets… James had no words. He squeezed the wheel. At only five thirty in the morning, the streets of the subdivision were relatively empty aside from the few joggers his headlights reflected off. He never thought he'd be so thankful for people who ran before work or the officer wouldn't have kept the driver of the sedan busy long enough for them to get away.

But where was the man that shot Rachel? She had her gaze glued to the side mirror. He pushed the van to as high a speed as he could control in the subdivision. "Did you see which way the man went after he shot you?"

"No. That's what worries me."

James tried to plan a route in his mind. He wanted to go north, toward his brother, David. As the owner of a large conference center on the beach, David had contacts throughout the vacation rental business. He only hoped David could arrange for them to rent one discreetly. Aria had sent him an email that it'd been too long since they'd seen each other and were hoping to visit soon. James hoped they didn't mind sooner than later.

David could take the boys somewhere off the grid. Rachel could stay in a beach house, and James could go straight to the FBI. The authorities might dismiss him as crazy since Launch Operations had all the necessary permits and the FBI didn't have jurisdiction, but James would have to take that chance. At the very least, everyone in his life would be safe again. Everyone except Derrick. *Please save him, Lord.*

Rachel faced forward. "Can I ask you a question?"

A glance in the rearview mirror showed the kids both wearing giant headphones. "Sure."

"Why'd you leave the NSA?"

Was she trying to change the subject? Or trying to keep her mind off the pain? "Because the private sector pays decent." He noticed her surprised expression, as if she'd never expected such a shallow answer from a deacon. "We both had school loans to pay, and even though we were never field operatives, it seemed safer to move on before kids."

It had been Nikki's idea to leave the NSA. At

first he wasn't sure it was the right move. He'd enjoyed going to work with his wife and he'd liked the security of having a government job with a serious cool factor. It wasn't until they'd found Launch Operations could employ them both for a whole lot more money and a schedule more conducive to family life that he'd gotten on board.

A week before Nikki passed away, she'd talked about quitting, suggested they search for a new line of work. She'd started acting jittery whenever a cabinet door closed or the boys cried. She'd called in sick, even though she'd seemed healthy.

He'd worried the time in the NSA had made her too paranoid to work on anything remotely dealing with government. He gritted his teeth together. What if her death wasn't an accident? Should he even let himself consider it? Hit-and-runs were on the rise. Statistically speaking, he had no reason to question it.

But if Launch Operations was hiding something and tried to use his boys as leverage to keep him quiet or to get him to help, what if they had done something similar before? It couldn't have been an electromagnetic pulse weapon, of course, but what if she'd discovered something else? Plans for the EMP? Something like this would've taken a lot of plotting. That was two years ago, though. What if she had found something else? Foreign spy capabilities attached to a satellite?

Nikki would have confided in him if that were the case, right? His head throbbed with the beginnings of a caffeine-withdrawal headache. He needed coffee. Besides, he knew the answer. If Nikki had come to him, he would've insisted on going to someone for help. He would've gone to Derrick just like he did now. What if Nikki had known a reason not to go to Derrick?

The whole scenario was ridiculous. He clung to the possibility so he'd no longer feel guilt for what had really happened that day. He'd forgotten to pick up the dry cleaning, which he said he'd do on the way home since she'd called in sick. Instead, Nikki had offered to go get it for him. He blinked at the memory, fighting against the pain gnawing at his chest. It was the same thought that had plagued him for the last two years: it should've been him.

"What'd you do for the NSA?"

Rachel's question snapped him out of his reflections. "I'm afraid I can't say any specifics, and it would probably bore your socks off anyway."

She looked so frail in the seat, gripping her shoulder. "Try me."

Fine. He'd humor her. "Data mining, algorithms, queries…"

"Queries? Like the type you do now?"

James tried not to let his surprise show that she understood some of his job at Launch Operations. She really had listened all those times she'd asked about work when they'd car-pooled.

"Uh, James?"

"Yeah?"

"It's still dark enough that the automatic headlights flipped on, right?"

"Yeah." They were about to turn out of the subdivision. So far there had been no sign of the police car. "Why? Do you think I should turn them off?"

"No." She pointed toward the passenger-side mirror. "I'm wondering why the black car a block behind us doesn't have them on."

TWELVE

Rachel knew why the car drove without lights, but she didn't want to admit it aloud.

James groaned. "I don't want to do this."

"Do what?"

He shot her an apologetic look. "Hold on." He shifted the van quickly and took the very next right turn.

Rachel pressed her back into the leather bucket seat, her wide eyes trained on the road ahead. Understanding hit her in the gut. She'd almost forgotten how his wife passed. James hated to drive fast or aggressively. She imagined if she'd had a loved one pass away from a hit-and-run she wouldn't, either. Her shoulder stung so bad, tears pricked her eyes.

He flicked on a turn signal and merged onto the freeway. They zoomed in and out of the few cars starting an early morning commute. "James, there's a second black sedan."

He cringed. "Even if we lose them, we're in trouble. They've seen the van."

"Silver vans are plentiful."

"Sure, but if we're dealing with NSA, any agent worth his salt would get a look at the license plate when it was sitting in the driveway. If they have any NSA resources—which we're still not sure about—they could track us easily."

Rachel jerked her head at the upcoming exit. "Take the next exit, James. We'll have a better chance of losing them off the freeway. Plus, it's not far to Eric's Automotive."

"Why?" He drove so fast they left the commuters in the dust. The streetlights reflected off the asphalt. Darkness and stars remained to the west, but in the mirror, behind the cars, the hints of a future sunrise played on the horizon.

"My vehicle is waiting to be worked on, remember? I had it towed there." Her insides twisted as she stared at her purse, which still held the gun. "We could switch license plates."

The black sedans were gaining on them. She kept her mouth closed as she noticed James glance at his mirror. He pursed his lips. "I like your thinking, but I'm worried they'd still recognize the make of the van. Eric's is still a good idea, though. I can work with that."

Crack!

A look in the rearview mirror confirmed a

man in one of the black sedan's sticking a gun out of the passenger-side window. "James!"

He swerved and kept swerving across the lanes. "I know!"

He continued driving in a winding path, like a snake weaving through blades of grass. While traffic would've really helped them hide, she was so thankful there weren't other cars to get hurt. It was all she could do not to black out. She planted her feet on either side of the floor mats to try to stay still without letting go of her shoulder.

He merged on the off-ramp without signaling, and all the lights within the van went off. "I turned off the interior and the headlights," he said. He took the first right, another right and a third right.

"We just went in a circle."

"I know." He pulled over to the side and two black sedans barreled down the main road.

"They didn't see us?"

James didn't answer but pulled out onto the road again, this time taking a left. They drove in tense silence. "What are you thinking?" she finally asked.

"How much I hate not having a phone. The first chance we get, I'm buying both of us phones and entering my family's phone numbers in them both."

"In mine?"

His expression looked grim. "I can't keep running with the boys like this, Rachel. Not with guns at play. If this doesn't work… If they find us again…" He took a deep breath. "If that happens, I'm going to pull over and step out with my hands up. You'll drive away with the boys and keep driving."

She shook her head, panicking. She couldn't be in charge of the boys. The responsibility was too great. She wasn't equipped. "I can barely drive like this."

"You'd just have to get to my parents'. Mom would take the boys and then you'd be free to go back to your life. These men want me. And, at this point, if push came to shove, I'd do what they wanted, if they just left you alone."

"James, who's to say they would let you leave after you do what they want? You'd be a liability." She didn't say what she was actually thinking: *they'll kill you.*

Judging by the set of his jaw, he was determined.

"You're not thinking straight." She tried again. "Besides, this is a moot point. We'll change the license plate and get somewhere safe. Together."

"We're not changing the plates. We're switching cars."

Though hard to see in the lightening darkness, a black sedan rounded the bend a couple blocks behind. "James, you have to speed up. They've spotted us." The last thing she needed was for him to give up now. She wanted to ask how he intended to change cars, but she couldn't tear her eyes away from the mirror.

"I see Eric's shop."

"They just drove through a light. It's definitely them. We need enough distance they won't see you pull in to the shop."

"I'm aware," he said. His voice held a twinge of desperation and anger.

The van lurched forward as he shifted into high gear. "Hold on, boys!" Rachel dared a look over their shoulder at their wide-eyed faces. Caleb flung off the headphones and Ethan mimicked him. "It's going to be okay," she said.

James zigzagged through a corner and darted behind Eric's Automotive where a couple of dozen cars sat, some with Used sticker prices on them and others presumably waiting to be worked on. Her maroon hybrid SUV sat in the line. She pointed. "Park next to it."

"I'm afraid they spotted where I turned." James shook his head.

"You are not giving up yet," Rachel insisted. "We have a few seconds. Park. I have an idea."

He flashed a look of unease.

"If it doesn't work, I'll follow your plan," Rachel added.

That did it. He swung into the spot.

"Grab the kids. I still have a spare key to my car. You'll hide underneath my cargo shelf. It's made for groceries, but the space underneath is plenty for the boys. You'll have to squish your legs, but they'll stay safe. In this lighting, it'll look like they're seeing the bottom of the trunk. All you'll see is gray."

He rolled his eyes, slammed the van into Park and jumped out of the van. They grabbed the boys. She clicked the fob and turned off the interior lights while he opened the trunk. "Hurry, hurry."

He slipped in flat and held his arms open for the boys to roll into each of his arms. Their heads grazed the top of the cargo privacy cover. "Shh, we're playing hide-and-seek," he whispered. His eyes met hers. "Where are you hiding?"

"Don't worry about me. Arms in." She slammed the trunk and darted around the side of a car. A hot sensation slid down her arm. Dark red splotches made a trail from the van to where she stood.

She gaped. The moment she'd let up pressure on her wound her blood had spilled onto the pavement. If the men looked closely, she'd have led them right to the boys' hiding spot.

Wheels crunched over the chip-sealed parking lot. Her breath quickened. Once they rounded the corner of the building, they'd see her. She hunched down and ran down the row of cars.

As she darted around the trunk of the last car, she found the trail had followed her. Good. She dropped to one knee and pulled off her blood-soaked hoodie, wiped off as much blood as she could, balled it up and threw it as far as she could with her good arm. It landed ten feet away in the field.

She sank down into a low squat so her head wouldn't be visible through the car windows. The wheels rolled over the asphalt steadily, slowly. Her right hand clamped down tightly on her wound. She made her way back toward her car on the headlight side of the cars, careful not to straighten lest they spot her.

The smell of oil and rubber tires triggered a headache. The crackling of tires against pavement slowed. A beam of light reflected off the side of one vehicle. She sank down to her knees and pulled out the gun from her purse. If they moved to open her trunk, she would step out and engage...if her shoulder didn't give way. Her heart raced at the thought of pointing a gun at a few men. If push came to shove, could she really pull the trigger?

A car door opened. "This is it," a gruff man's voice said. "Their stuff is still in it. Looks like they took off, though." Another car door opened and shut. Their feet sounded so close. Where were they? If they rounded the vehicle and saw her first, she'd lose the advantage of surprise.

"Think they left on foot?"

Something shifted. Was it from the car or from the men? *Please help those boys stay quiet, Lord.*

"Look. Blood."

"That'd be my handiwork," the man replied. Rachel could almost picture his smug face. Her finger slipped to the trigger of the gun.

A beam of light searched the field behind her. Rachel molded herself against the wheel.

"The trail takes off into the field. Looks like her jacket caught on something. Let's check those office buildings just past it. They couldn't have gotten far."

The car doors closed. Wait, they were going to drive right past her. She'd be spotted even if she stayed in a squat position.

Rachel dove to the pavement and rolled underneath the car, praying the darkness would cover her shadow. The rocks bit into her shoulder. She sucked in a breath. Without the hooded sweatshirt to cushion the movement she almost cried out. Hot tears rolled down her face. Her lips quivered as she held her breath.

Tires sped off. She finally exhaled, a strangled cry escaping from the agony pulsating within her shoulder. She remained frozen for a few minutes, breathing the horrible oil fumes underneath her vehicle. The creaking and groaning coming from the car likely meant the boys had tired of staying still.

She tucked the gun back into her purse before she sniffed and wiped the tears away with her right hand. Shimmying her way out from under the vehicle was even more difficult as little bits of asphalt pressed into her skull, hands and hips.

She sat up into a crouch position and brushed off the stinging bits embedded in her skin. In the distance she heard the cars, but they still had their lights off. She waited until she couldn't see them before she clicked the fob to unlock her vehicle.

Her right arm struggled with her weight as she tried to push herself up to standing.

James had popped open the trunk from the inside. He sat up, the boys wiggling free from his arms. "Worst game of hide-and-seek ever," he muttered.

"Let's hope we never have to play it again."

Ethan's eyes bulged as he pointed at her. "She bleeding."

James pulled off his sweatshirt and handed it to her. "It needs pressure."

She pressed it against the wound. "Every time I move it starts back up again."

"Then we need to get you somewhere you can stay put."

If only.

He jumped out of the vehicle and pointed to a crummy white van near the office doors. "I helped Eric out a time or two. He leaves the loaner available for anyone who needs to drop off their car after hours." He jogged back to the minivan and pulled out the two booster seats. "Let's go."

"But what about the keys?"

He shrugged. "I'm hoping the hiding place is the same as last time. You have a pen in your purse?"

"I think so." She moved to rummage.

"Please let me." James reached for the strap on her left shoulder. His fingers brushed against the curve of her neck and she released a small gasp. "Did I hurt you?"

She blushed. "No." Her right hand helped him remove the purse off her torso. He found the pen in record time. He ripped off one of the sales papers attached to the side of a car and jotted a quick note to Eric.

Emergency. Had to take your loaner. Out of touch for a bit. Will pay whatever you ask for inconvenience.
Sorry,
James McGuire.

He slipped the note through the mail slot in the glass door and found the key right where he'd found it last, underneath the back right tire well. A minute later, he kept the lights off while they drove back onto the freeway.

Rachel found a baseball cap with the repair shop's logo on it in the back. She hunkered down below the window on the chance they were spotted.

He merged onto the freeway and exhaled. "I think you can sit up."

She straightened, rolling her shoulders back and dropping her chin to her chest. "Thanks," she groaned, continuing to get the kinks out. "Next stop, coffee?"

He laughed. "I wish. Let's get out of town, and let me look at your wound. I'm still not convinced we shouldn't take you to a hospital."

"Can we walk through some hypotheticals?"

Oh, how that word was music to his ears. Hypotheticals. "Of course."

"Say we get these burner phones. If we are dealing with some NSA guys, can't they still track them?"

"Theoretically, yes, but in a practical sense, no. Landline and cell phones registered on a certain network can be immediately traced, but prepaid phones take a while longer. They can't easily be pinpointed to an exact location."

She rubbed her eyes and yawned. "Why is that?"

"Phone companies have an interface that is configured to deliver activity to law enforcement on request. They would need to call the company and set up a trace on all incoming calls from certain numbers—assuming they could figure out certain parameters and key words to filter which ones would be coming from us—then they would ping the phone numbers to find the closest call station."

She smiled. "So it's unlikely they'll track us if you use the burner. Finally some good news."

He nodded. "Unless they are tracing the person I'm calling. Then it'll be a piece of cake."

Her face dropped. "Oh."

"That would take a while. It's why I think calling my parents might be riskier than calling my brother. If it's NSA, it's likely they've been monitoring who I usually call."

"Your mom," she answered. "You call her every week."

He nodded. "Which is a bummer because Mom used to be a detective. She would have the best chance of leading me to someone else we could trust. But, I hardly ever call my brother, and I'm going to take care not to use any trigger words. I won't be explaining any of our situation."

The boys grew quiet. In the rearview mirror he found they'd fallen asleep. Long car rides could always be counted for that. He took the exit for the next small town and pulled into a store parking lot. "Do you mind waiting in the car?"

She looked down at his blood-soaked sweatshirt. "Under the circumstances, that's probably a good idea." She nodded toward her purse. "Could you hand me the gun?"

He did so, and she slipped it underneath her leg for quick access. James checked his cash. It was less than he thought. Eighty-dollars should get him a couple of burner phones, but would it cover the first-aid supplies and food he'd need to purchase, as well?

"Take the cash in my purse."

"I will not."

She rolled her eyes. "It's my grocery and entertainment money for the next two weeks. It's not much, but combined with yours it should get us what we need."

"Fine, but it's a loan."

"I know where you live," she joked, but her eyes were closed. Pain radiated across her face.

He pointed to her shoulder. "Let me look." She slid the bundled-up sweatshirt down. The bleeding had slowed considerably, but a giant gash ran diagonally across her shoulder. He huffed. "Ideally, you probably need stitches."

"We'll just bandage it up as best as we can. I'm not afraid of scars."

He pulled back. How many scars did she carry internally from her childhood? He nodded. "I'll be fast. Leave without me if there's any sign of them. Promise?"

She rolled her eyes. "Fine."

He stepped out of the van.

"Snacks and caffeine will help the pain," she called after him.

James ran across the mostly empty parking lot to the store. He didn't want to leave Rachel alone much longer in the van. While her affection for the boys seemed obvious, she'd grown jumpy around them, second-guessing everything she said. Was it because he'd tried to kiss her? He'd really messed up there. If there were ever an award for Most Awkward Running-For-Your-Life Road Trip, he'd take the prize.

James made short work of the shopping. He held the two grocery bags and two paper cups as he scanned the parking lot for the white van. Approaching, he quickened his step. He couldn't see Rachel. Coffee sloshed from his cup and foam ran down the other. He spotted the top of her head and exhaled.

The sun peeked over the horizon, a dazzling display of colors that highlighted her dark eyelashes and pink lips. The same lips that laughed at his weak attempts at humor, that challenged him, that spoke the words that would give him chills for the rest of his life. *You will not touch those boys.* And the same lips that had brushed against his even for half a second.

The woman was fearless…except when it came to him. Maybe she didn't fear him. Perhaps she just feared rejecting him and what that would do to their friendship. The thought struck him. Were they more than just neighbors? Were they friends?

She pointed with her right hand to his head. "Bought a hat?"

"Yeah. We can trade if you want the newer one."

"Nah." Her eyes drifted to his hands. "Coffee," she said as if it was a long-lost love.

He offered it to her. "Grande, salted caramel mocha, half the syrup, extra hot. Is that right?"

She gasped, reaching with her right hand. "I love y—" Her eyes flickered to his face, and a deep blush spread across her cheeks. Her tone had been playful until she'd clearly remembered his attempt to kiss her.

Now it was his turn to be embarrassed.

"I love that drink," she amended.

She took a long sip as he got adjusted in the seat. She cried out when he applied the antiseptic to her shoulder, and the boys stirred. Her face crumpled. "I'm sorry."

"Don't be. They're probably hungry." He handed the boys some breakfast bars, juice boxes and a cheap electronic game he'd purchased.

The adhesive skin closures he bought barely held her wound. They looked weak and about to break with the slightest movement. He grimaced.

There was something else he could do, though. "This is going to seem so weird, Rachel, but I've seen it work on remote construction sites."

He reached into the shopping bag for the duct tape and travel sewing kit he'd picked up, just in case. He tore off two one-inch pieces of duct tape, folded down the long side of each one and placed them on either side of her wound.

"Wh-what are you doing?" She pointed at the travel sewing kit as he threaded a needle.

"I'm going through the duct tape, not your skin." He exhaled. "But it's not going to feel good."

Fear flickered in her eyes, but she nodded and looked away.

His fingers moved quickly, sewing through the folded-over portions of the duct tape. He pulled the strings to pull the duct tape, and therefore her skin, tight together. "There. That seems more secure. It'll at least hold until we can get you somewhere for real stitches."

Rachel blew out a breath as he tied the knot. She turned to him and tears threatened to spill down her cheeks. It broke his heart. He wanted to reach for her and pull her close.

Instead he dove back into the first-aid supplies he'd purchased and covered his sewing work with a large bandage. "I'm so sorry, Rachel."

She sniffed. "Don't be. You didn't shoot me. You patched me up. Thank you."

He had no words, so he turned the van back on so he could get the phones charging before they left.

Her finger traced the outside of her coffee lid. "You didn't order the same thing, did you?"

"No, plain coffee does it for me." The plastic

packaging on the phones wouldn't budge. What kind of plastic was this? They should make internal components out of it. Unbreakable.

"How'd you know to order this drink, then? It's pretty specific."

He looked up. Oh, she was still talking about the coffee. "Most Wednesdays you have a decaf version of one of those in your hands at church." He threw a thumb toward the white-printed label on the side.

She flashed a dazzling smile. "I suppose I do." Her eyes drifted to the phone packaging. She set the drink in the cup holder and unzipped her purse. The sight of the gun under her leg reminded him to be on guard. They needed to get back on the road.

She pulled out a pair of scissors and slid the blades out of a protective shield. He reached for them and she shook her head. "Could you just hold out the package? These blades are ridiculously expensive."

He frowned but held it steady. "How much?"

"You don't want to know," she mumbled. As if performing a delicate operation, she barely nicked the packaging with only a half inch of the blades.

"Why do you have them in your purse?"

"They're an extra pair of shears I keep with

me. A couple weekends a month I give haircuts outside of the salon."

"To anyone?"

She sighed as she made tiny cuts to the plastic. "To women about to go on job interviews."

In other words, she helped the women at the shelter the church sponsored. James didn't want to embarrass her, but it only strengthened his opinion of her.

He was able to get the phones up and running within minutes. Despite her protest, James entered his family members' phone numbers and his parents' address into the phone he'd purchased for her. "Just in case," he added. "Wherever we stay, it's going to be north and this—" he threw a thumb over his shoulder at the content boys "—won't last much longer."

He pulled back onto the freeway, headed to the coastal 101 highway. Once on the road, he dialed David's number. "Pick up, pick up," James muttered.

"Hello?"

"David." Relief coursed through his veins. "It's James. I was worried you wouldn't pick up."

"I wasn't going to, but Aria worried it was one of the employees calling. You got a new number?"

"For a short time." James wanted to keep the

conversation as short as possible. "I'm hoping you can help me."

"If I can, I will. Name it."

"Please use your connections to find me a beach house in Northern California for a day or two, starting today. I know it's short notice but—"

"How about Central California coast instead?"

"Uh, yeah. That'd probably be even better." He had assumed David's connections were closer to the conference center he ran on the Oregon Coast, but he wasn't complaining.

"I know just the place."

"That's not all. I need to use cash."

"Won't be a problem. People who deal with me are used to it. You know how Dad drilled into us the—"

James didn't have time for a budget lesson refresher. "Could you call me back once you've got a place?"

"No need. Can you get to Pismo Beach?"

James felt his eyes widen. That was closer than he'd imagined. It'd still take a few hours, but it'd suit his needs. "That'd be perfect. Are you sure you can get it?"

"Positive." David rattled off the address. James repeated it, and Rachel typed it with one hand into the notepad of her charging smartphone. "The door will be open, or I'll make sure there is a key under the mat."

"I have another huge favor to ask," James said. "I need you to be on call in case I need you to come and take the boys somewhere for a few days. I'm hoping that won't be necessary, but I'm covering my bases."

His huge request was met with a pause. "Are you in some kind of trouble?"

"You could say that, but I can't go into details right now. I hope to have it all fixed in a few days."

"Is it the kind of trouble Aria and I had to deal with?"

He cringed. He hadn't witnessed a murder by the Russian mafia with an impending tsunami on his heels, so, no. "You can't really compare the two."

"Or Luke and Gabriella?"

He didn't want to say the word "mafia" over the phone lest it trigger any kind of NSA tracking, but he couldn't really compare his situation with theirs, either. "Completely different."

"Good. Because Mom was starting to worry she'd raised four danger-seeking vigilantes."

James considered the absurd possibility. "Maybe danger comes to us and not the other way around."

David laughed. "That's what I said!"

"David, do me a favor and don't tell anyone about this conversation." He hung up before his brother could respond. He'd just add it to the list of apologies he'd owe everyone if they ever got out of this situation.

THIRTEEN

Rachel studied every car that crossed their path. Every dark sedan made her flinch.

James twisted the radio dial. He stopped at a Celine Dion song. "Hey. You like this one."

She gaped at him. She adored listening to Celine Dion songs while she swept or mopped. It was something Meredith used to do, and they would both dramatically sing and dance around the house while they cleaned. "Do…do you like Celine Dion?"

"Uh, not really. But I know you like her."

"How?" Her mouth hung open. Had he been spying on her?

"If you don't want the neighborhood to know you like Celine Dion, you should probably close your windows when you're cleaning." His eyes darted her way and his lips curved upward to one side as if fighting a laugh.

"Oh." She sank back into her seat. The whole

neighborhood? She did have a habit of belting it out...

"You like this song, huh, Rachel?" a little voice piped up from the back.

James didn't fight the laugh any longer.

"Okay," Rachel said. "I guess you know that about me, but I also know you guys have a wrestling event every night before bed."

He froze. "Oh?"

"Yes, the boys are always Caleb and Ethan but with fun adjectives added to their name, but yours are always so creative. I believe you've been..." She racked her brain to remember the names he'd call out in a deep voice. "The Gorilla. The Clown. The BoomBoom. The Hammer..."

His entire face flushed. "Point taken."

She grinned in triumph. "If you don't want the neighborhood to know..."

"Yeah, yeah," he acknowledged. "I often close the blinds, but with the nice weather..."

"Me, too." She closed her blinds when she cleaned, too, but left the windows open. It was easy to forget that the whole world could still hear you when they couldn't see you. "I suppose we know more about each other than I thought just by being neighbors."

He nodded then raised an eyebrow. "Why? What else do you know?"

"Nothing bad. I know that you grill almost all the time, even in the winter."

"Hmm." He pushed the hair falling over his eyes back. "What else?"

"And you keep a freakishly perfect yard."

"Well, that's just being a good neighbor."

She sighed as she watched his handsome profile. If falling for him didn't mean being a mom... But even if she ever did get over that, what would it be like to be with someone who'd already been married to the love of his life? Could a crippled heart love fully?

"Let's see. I know you go on lots of dates," James said. "I see the guys pick you up, but you never invite them in, not even for a few minutes. So, either you don't want them to see your house because you're not a tidy person—which after seeing the inside yesterday doesn't seem likely—or you fiercely guard your heart."

She felt her face fall. The humor disappeared as fast as it appeared. She narrowed her eyes. "Are you trying to ask why I said—" She darted a look to see the boys occupied with their cheap electronic game before diving into the topic of why she couldn't be with him.

He shrugged. "No. Just an observation."

She held up a hand. "I think that was more than an observation." It felt like more of an attack, except, if she looked at the facts alone, it was one hundred percent true. His tone, though, said more. "You know, if you had asked me why I can't be in a relationship with you, I would've told you," she said softly.

"I don't need to ask why. I'm sure you had your reasons." His shoulders dropped. "I want to respect your decision."

She said nothing but something inside softened. Of all the men she'd dated—and there were a lot—no one had said they respected her decision. "Is it because you have your own reasons?" she blurted. "Is that why you didn't ask?"

"Does it matter?" He kept his eyes plastered on the road, not paying her a single glance. "If it's not right, it's not right. Why torture ourselves?"

She nodded. It made sense. She looked out the side window. He had a point. Leave it alone. It was a wise, logical decision… She turned back to him. "Because it's going to drive me crazy if I don't know."

He sighed. "Okay. Well, there is the obvious…we're neighbors."

"Yeah. That was my thinking, too." She tried to relax in her seat. That was all. A tingling in the back of her neck wouldn't let it go. "But… the way you said that implies there's more."

He pursed his mouth. Did he keep making

those expressions—the ones that drew her eyes to his lips—to show her what she'd missed? To remind her she could've kissed him?

She focused on her hands as she waited for his reply. Bloodstains remained underneath her nails on her right hand. It served as a reminder that they may not even get through the weekend alive.

"My heart broke when I lost Nikki," James said. "I don't know if it'll ever be whole again so I don't want to risk further damage by someone who has any doubts. And I imagine—no one could blame you—that the fact I come with two kids as a package deal and find social situations excruciating makes me not the best fit for someone like you." He cringed, as if replaying his own words and not approving. "Have I put your mind to rest?"

"Almost."

"This is more talking than I do in a typical day."

She ignored that. "What did you mean 'someone like me'?"

"I don't know, like *you*." He emphasized the last word as if it made it all clear. "Beautiful, kind, funny, smart, an extrovert…"

He thought she was smart? She blinked and faced forward. "Oh."

The awkwardness of the conversation combined with Celine Dion's love ballads playing in the background made her squirm in her seat. Rachel raised her cup to her lips only to realize there wasn't any latte left.

"Wh-what about you?" James asked softly.

She raised her eyebrows. "Me?"

He bobbed his head side to side. "You said you agreed with the neighbors part, but the way *you* said it also sounded like there was more to it."

"Oh." Rachel stared at the van ceiling hoping a Pull to Eject switch would suddenly appear. She *had* said she would tell him if he asked. She inhaled. "Well, I told you I had a bad childhood..."

He nodded.

"I never had a good example in parenting. And I watched my friends, who grew up in the same sort of environment, have kids and raise them in the exact same horrible ways, and that's when I knew. I could never be a mom. I wouldn't want to treat kids the way I was treated, and I think, judging by what I've seen, that it would be unavoidable." She waited for his response, sure he would understand.

He frowned, as if processing. "That's ridiculous."

Her jaw dropped. Not the reaction she'd expected at all. "Excuse me?"

"That's like saying a kid who grows up with horrible teeth, riddled with tons of cavities, shouldn't be a dentist."

"I think it's a little more complicated than that, James." She flinched at how harsh she'd said his name.

"Okay, well… What about Eleanor Roosevelt?" He gestured with one hand. "She had a pretty bad childhood from what I can gather and was known for being a good mother to her six children and a champion of those who were oppressed."

Was that true? Something warm flared in her chest. "I've never heard that, but you're a guy who loves math and statistics. Surely you can see the statistics for being a good mother aren't in my favor."

"What I see is a woman who cares enough that it wouldn't be an issue. Even people with great childhoods, like me for example, still struggle to be a good parent. It's just hard no matter what. And for the record, the way you were willing to sacrifice yourself for Caleb and Ethan—" His voice shook. "I think a woman willing to do that could be a good mom if she wanted."

He adjusted his ball cap up and down as if he couldn't find a comfortable position for it over that full head of hair. "Um, I'm not implying that… I mean, I'm not arguing for you…" He cleared his throat. "To be clear, I'm not trying to convince you to mother my children. Not at all."

He didn't make eye contact. He stared straight ahead and gestured forward with one hand, as if helping him to stay on track. "I get that I'm not the guy, Rachel. That's not my point. If I had my wish, we'd go back twenty minutes ago and avoid this conversation."

"I know." Her voice barely came out as a squeak.

He sighed. "I've handled this so badly I can't even begin to apologize, Rachel. First, I—I tried to kiss you," he said. "And I didn't even ask your permission or ask you on a date…and then I practically belittled you for what is probably a very wise decision. It wasn't my intent, but I know it probably came out that way."

"You saw the failed logic." It was her turn to speak in monotone.

"I saw the holes in the logic," he said, much softer. "In an otherwise fearless woman, it seemed incongruent. It didn't take in account any feelings, convictions or, most importantly, prayer. I've been operating on steam and acting insensitive. Please forgive me."

It wasn't a question. It was a petition. Add that to the long list of things no one had asked her before, for forgiveness. And while her thoughts still swam with everything he said, it was a no-brainer. "I will."

The air around them felt electric, as though a spotlight had been shining on them for the past hour inside a counselor's office with no exit. He thought she was fearless? She huffed at the thought. It couldn't be further from the truth at the moment. She sighed, slightly worried where any more thinking or talking might take them.

Except for a quick stop at a gas station, he drove as fast as the speed limit allowed. On little sleep, the hours driving in silence seemed like they'd never end. James tried to block out the conversation with Rachel, but it played on a loop in his mind. The rolling hills, the stretches of fog and the gorgeous silver-blue ocean water in the distance all fought for his attention, but it didn't work. He'd never intended to talk about the kiss that barely happened, but in the event he did, he'd never imagined it having gone so poorly. How did a guy recover from something like that?

"Why do you think the risk will be over once we get past Sunday?" Rachel asked. "You said the launch is scheduled for then, right? Won't they still need you?"

"No. Scheduling a launch is incredibly complicated. They can't just change the date without doing significant figures and program modifications. The processes I wrote will only stall the launch on Sunday. After that they can reschedule a launch with no problem."

"Why? Won't your virus still be hindering them?"

He shook his head. "I wrote the process with the orbital values in mind. If they change the launch, they have to change the orbit, which will render my work void. But they will want to do everything possible to not reschedule. It'll shine more attention on what they're doing, and the permits will need to be updated. They'll have to request recertification."

"So we're just going to wait it out, and then?"

"I haven't thought that far," he admitted. "I'm still praying Derrick pulls through and can help us out. If not, I pray God makes it obvious what I'm supposed to do." He exhaled a giant breath of air. "I'm sorry. It's all I've got."

"It's better than nothing."

The sign for Pismo Beach prompted him to slow down and turn on his left-turn signal. "We're almost there." And now he would be spending time, alone, in a big beach house with the boys and Rachel. Yeah, it wasn't going to be awkward at all.

Rachel told him to take yet another left. She'd

pulled up the address on her burner phone. Without a map, he would have driven in circles around the tourist area. It was still early in spring so the Spring Break craze had yet to begin. So far the side streets were empty of both people and vehicles.

"Take the next left."

James studied the layout of the neighborhood. "David got us a place on the southern end."

"That's good?"

He nodded. "Away from the restaurants and closer to the secluded dunes."

She pointed at the single-story California Craftsman surrounded by palm trees. "This must be it. It looks huge."

He parked on the side of the street next to three pickup trucks. Seemed a bit odd in this area to have so many oversize pickups, the type his brothers and dad were so fond of in the construction and housing business. Usually he saw more fuel-efficient vehicles. "Okay, time to gather our things."

She popped open the console between them. He stared at the gun resting inside. Would he still need it?

"Take it," she urged. "You might want to go ahead of us and check it out. Just in case."

He slipped the gun underneath his shirt as

he looked over his shoulder to make sure the boys were occupied with the Silly Putty he'd purchased in a gas station. He groaned as he saw strings of it stuck in their hair. "Add that to my list of great ideas," he muttered.

She followed his gaze and cracked a smile. "It's fine. I can get that right out with a little conditioner or baby oil."

What would I do without you? The words were on the tip of his tongue. He almost said it but, thankfully, he'd finally regained control of his tongue.

Rachel opened the van door, and the breeze made her shiver. She pulled on his sweatshirt. Bloodstains decorated the front and back. She cringed. "I hope no one sees me like this."

They formed a line as they walked on the sidewalk leading to the back of the house… or in this case, the front of the house, which faced the beach.

He pointed to a palm tree and told Rachel and the boys to wait for him to check it out. He rounded the corner and placed a hand on his stomach, ready to grab the weapon if needed. The crash of ocean tides made it hard to listen for warning signs as he stepped closer to peek into the windows.

Heat rushed to his face. Sitting on two couches

were two of his brothers, their wives and his mom and dad.

He was going to kill David.

David jumped up from the couch at the sight of him. "You're here," he hollered.

"What is it?" Rachel stepped backward into the shadow of the palm trees, holding Caleb's hand in her right and Ethan's hand in her left.

"It's fine," James muttered. Though it wasn't.

David opened the sliding-glass door. "Hey."

"What are you trying to pull?" James demanded.

David held up both hands. "You asked for a beach house. You didn't ask for an empty one."

"You knew what I meant."

"We were already here. You just never asked."

James tried to digest that little tidbit. "You guys went on vacation without me?" He shook his head. That wasn't the point. "None of you should be here."

David raised an eyebrow. "Why?" His eyes drifted over James's head and onto Rachel. His mouth hung open for half a second. "Uh. What's going on, bro?"

"I'm afraid your little omission has put you all in danger." James said it softly so no one else would hear.

"Uncle David," the twins cried. They wrenched free from Rachel's grasp and ran toward David.

"Then it means *you're* in danger," David said. "And from where I stand, that makes it a good thing we're here." He took a knee just as the boys reached him and opened his arms wide for a giant hug.

Aria, Luke, Gabriella, Mom and Dad all piled through the door, attacking his boys and him with hugs and exclamations. "Guys, guys, we need to get inside," James tried to argue. He looked over his shoulder and grimaced. "Rachel, meet my family."

FOURTEEN

Rachel's heart pounded fast, which made her shoulder throb painfully. His family was here?

James accepted a one-armed hug from one of the men as he waved her forward. One man shared the same tall, streamlined build as James, except with a full head of dark blond hair. While the first one—David, she thought the boys called him—was built like a lean football player with wavy hair. The older man was somewhere in between the two types with silver hair. All in all, the McGuire men made a handsome crew.

The older woman's hair, pulled back in a loose chignon, looked most like David's with its copper highlights. The other two women were both gorgeous but very different. One blonde, one dark brunette, they both had smiles that could light up a town.

The older woman's eyes met Rachel. She smiled the same way James did, a smile that seemed genuine and friendly, but before she could say anything the dad caught her gaze. "Whoa, son, what do we have here?" he asked.

Rachel's entire body burned with embarrassment. What must they think? A romantic getaway? She wasn't that type of girl, and she almost said it aloud. She stepped out of the shadows of the palm tree and approached them.

"Dad, stop," James said. "There's been an attempted...several actually..." He patted the top of the twins' heads while he mouthed the word, *kidnappings.* "It's a long story, but Rachel's my neighbor and because of me, she's also been targeted. We need a place to lay low."

His mom walked out of the pack and put her hands on Rachel's shoulders. "I don't know what happened, but my boys seem to have a knack for getting beautiful girls into danger."

"Mom—" Two of the brothers started to object in unison.

"I apologize for all of them," the mom said, ignoring her sons. She studied Rachel and paled. "Are you bleeding? What happened?"

James stepped closer. "She was shot, Mom. I tried to patch her up, but I'd appreciate it if you took a look."

His mom's jaw dropped. "Inside now. Everyone."

They stepped inside a beige kitchen with a

large round table for eight. The twins took off running through the house, eager to be out of the car. The rest of the family introduced themselves and Rachel tried her best to commit their names to memory.

She sat still while James explained the entire situation to his family. His mom checked her son's handiwork. "Unorthodox, but this should heal nicely. We need to watch for infection, though."

Gabriella rushed in with a clean cotton jacket for Rachel. The men remained impassive as James finished his recap. They listened, nodded and asked the occasional question. Aria and Gabriella kept looking at Rachel with wide eyes but said nothing.

His mom, who chose a seat directly to her right, grabbed Rachel's forearm each time James mentioned the men who chased them. "You saved the boys," she whispered.

All the attention was enough to drive Rachel batty. She needed space, time to think…

"You need a plan," his mom cried.

"Mom, the plan is to wait it out so I don't put any more family members in danger." James sent a pointed look in David's direction. "What I'd really like to know right now is why my entire family is taking vacations without me."

"Oh, please. This isn't a vacation," his mom

replied. "We were already here when you called for your brother's business. Tell him, David."

"We were already here when you called. It's how I had the address handy." David placed his elbows on the table. "There's a property here that's about to go up for auction."

James leaned back, the surprise evident on his face. "You're ready to start another conference center?"

"It's why I asked Dad and Luke to join us. I wanted a contractor and a real-estate developer's opinion."

"What, you didn't need Matt? Isn't he managing a conference center in San Antonio?"

Luke stretched one arm around his wife's shoulders. "He couldn't get away."

James shook his head. "I see how it is."

Rachel didn't realize he was the only one in the family that didn't have a job somehow related to the rest of his family. And, she hadn't heard about Matt, but the other two brothers had wives. Judging by how close the couples sat to each other, they were very much in love. Did James feel like an outsider in his own family?

Aria leaned forward. "James, we didn't call you because your mom told us you had a launch scheduled. We know how crazy it gets."

"We were going to ask you on Tuesday to come spend a couple days with us," his mom added. "I know you can never leave before a launch. And if I'd asked you beforehand or told you about it, you'd be stressed, feeling like you were missing out or disappointing us. Am I right?"

James rolled his eyes. "Maybe."

She frowned. "Which brings us back to your situation. You need a plan."

James slapped a hand on the table. "Sunday is the launch. Since you're here, I'll leave the boys and Rachel with you and take the risk of going to the authorities. But I'm praying Derrick recovers before then. You guys need to pretend we're not here, but you also need to stop using your phones." He pointed at the windows. "I should be watching. Someone always needs to be on the lookout."

"Phones," Rachel repeated. "James, we should call Cynthia."

He raised his eyebrows. "I didn't want to argue with Cynthia at the time, but it's still kind of risky to call her. They might be tracking her phone."

"Didn't you say a prepaid is harder to track? Besides, she said she wouldn't even answer if she didn't have news." Rachel hated the thought of sitting around, waiting. If Derrick had pulled through his surgery, Cynthia could relay information, maybe even tell them what to do…

James stood and paced, peeking through the front windows at the road. "I'd want to get far away from here before I do that. Just to be safe."

David glanced at his smartphone. "We actually have a meeting. How about you let us take the boys? There are some sand dunes and a giant golf course they could run around on. The boys can give us an opinion if kids would like the place."

Uncertainty crossed his features. "I'm not—"

"You said it yourself. No one knows you're here. And you've got two uncles, two aunts and a grandpa standing guard who would do anything for them," his dad said.

"I'll stay here with Rachel," his mom added. She patted Rachel's hand. "We'll get to know each other and get the rooms ready for you guys. I imagine you'll want to call it a night early. You look like you could fall asleep standing up."

"You have no idea, Mom."

The family moved as one, everyone standing up and getting ready to leave. The boys squealed in excitement when Uncle Luke asked them if they wanted to go run on sand dunes. Within moments the house quieted as everyone left.

Rachel's heart pounded in her throat. James was going to leave her here with his mom? She tried to send a signal to James by widening her eyes, but when he looked at her he just smiled.

"Dad, I'm borrowing your beach hat." He picked up a floppy brown hat that looked ridiculous. It certainly worked as a disguise. "I'm going to walk a couple miles south and call Cynthia. Mom, keep watch," he said and walked out the door.

"So you're the neighbor," his mom said. "I've heard loads about you."

Ah, the Sunday phone chats James had told her about. Wasn't his mom the one that advised they stop car-pooling? So that meant she knew Rachel dated other men. Did that mean she automatically didn't like her? Did she think she was taking advantage of James for the gas savings? Rachel jiggled her knee up and down, trying to release the anxiety, trying to focus her thoughts.

"The boys and James speak very highly of you."

The sun streaming in through the windows heated her to the core. At least, she told herself it was the sun's fault.

"Want to keep me company while I start on dinner?"

"I think I better keep a lookout, Mrs. McGuire."

"Call me Beverly. You can do both at the same time."

"I've got just a great taco bake recipe on my

tablet." Beverly propped up her tablet on the counter. The screensaver displayed a slide show of pictures of her boys then wedding photos... including a photo of James and Nikki. The boys had Nikki's bright smile and blond hair.

Beverly caught her gaze. "It took me over a year before I could put that picture back in the slideshow, but Nikki was the type of woman who wouldn't want us to wallow forever. She will always be missed." Beverly took a deep breath. "But I know she'd have wanted James to find a partner in parenting the boys. She'd want what was best for all three of them."

Rachel wanted to run out of the room. It was likely her imagination, but it was almost as if Beverly was insinuating...

"Of course, I'd never push James," Beverly continued. "I'm not one of those meddling moms. My friends think I should give him a little nudge, but that seems a bit much, don't you think? No, matchmaking doesn't suit me one bit."

While a relief Beverly didn't want to interfere, the entire topic made her uneasy. The slide show switched to a family photo of all the boys and their parents. "You must be very proud," Rachel said, hoping she'd switch subjects.

Beverly put her hands on her hips and nodded. "Yes, by God's grace."

"Sure, but you can take some credit. You made sure they had a good start," Rachel added.

Beverly studied her with a sharp eye before she swiped the tablet and pulled up the recipe. "My own parents divorced at age five. Tim also came from a broken home. We had parents who loved us but made mistakes, just as every parent does. I'd like to think we gave them a good start, but in the end, like I said, it's by God's grace."

"How'd you make sure they grew up better than you?"

Beverly laughed. "Oh, we could never have guaranteed that. Each of the boys was so different. Even if I had the best parents, the best childhood, the best parenting books, I'd still have been on my knees asking Him for wisdom."

Rachel stared at the recipe and tried to contain her surprise. It was hard to imagine Mrs. McGuire not knowing what to do in all situations.

Beverly tapped her finger on the countertop. "He gently leads those that have young. I found that somewhere in Isaiah once. I clung to it because it meant that motherhood wasn't all on me." Beverly moved around the kitchen, preparing ingredients.

"I'm sure your experience as a cop had to come in handy with parenting," Rachel said.

Beverly chuckled and moved to brown the beef on the stovetop. "I suppose some of the skills I developed helped in raising boys." She waved the wooden spatula in the air. "The power of observation helped the most. Detective work."

"I wouldn't have anything like that to draw on," she said.

Beverly let the spatula rest on the side of the pan and turned to her. "It doesn't matter. Don't let your past stop you from a future God may call you to eventually. There are a lot of motherless in this world." She held up both hands. "Don't misunderstand me. My grandchildren will be just fine. I'm no matchmaker." Beverly winked at Rachel.

Rachel felt her eyes widen and tried not to make eye contact.

A shadow crossed the deck. Rachel reached for the gun in her purse, slung across the back of a kitchen chair. James appeared at the glass door, and she exhaled. He slid open the door and stepped in, his face grim. "Bad news. Cynthia never answered."

"It doesn't mean Derrick's not okay," she said. Her encouraging words didn't move the weight that had dropped in the pit of her stomach.

James nodded, but his head hung low. The strain of not knowing if his friend would live or die had to hurt. He removed the gigantic beach hat from his head. "You guys doing okay here?"

Rachel glanced at Mrs. McGuire. That was a loaded question.

Loud talking came from the side of the house. James rushed to the side of the door and waited. His gun rested in the back of his jeans. The moment he recognized David's voice he relaxed and stepped away but not before his mom's concerned gaze met his. "I don't even know if we should be here." He ran his hand through his hair. The last thing he wanted was to bring any more of his loved ones into danger.

"This is exactly where you should be," she answered.

The rest of the family entered. Luke held Caleb, and David carried Ethan. Everyone was talking over each other, the noise almost deafening. Rachel crossed the room, peering out the windows. His family was sure to draw attention at this volume.

A shrill whistle echoed through the room, the vaulted ceiling echoing it. James turned to find everyone staring at Mom.

"Since when did you know how to do that?" David asked, incredulous.

Mom shrugged. "Gabriella taught me. Now, James, I'm going to take a look at my network to see who you should contact."

"I told you, Mom, I'm waiting until Sunday."

Mom raised her eyebrows and blinked slowly, obviously irritated. "Fine. When's the launch?"

"Eleven p.m. GMT NET." They always announced launch times in GMT. The number stuck in his head more than the actual time.

"What?" Rachel asked.

"Greenwich Mean Time," James clarified. "No earlier than." He put a hand on his head, mentally calculating when that would be. "Uh, that's 4:00 p.m. Pacific time, Sunday."

"James, that's tomorrow. You need to talk to someone now," Mom said. "I don't know who I can get on a Sunday so we need to get right to it…I'll need to make some calls."

"Mom, that's the one thing you can't do."

"If you don't stop this in time—"

"Don't you think I know that?" Every muscle tensed in his back. He should've known he'd get pushback from Mom. "I know the facts, and the risks. The satellite has to make a full orbit, coming up from the south, before it gets in any place to do any damage to our electrical infrastructure. If I can reach someone after launch that's still time for the air force to shoot it down before it gets near the target."

"You know your world, James, but I know law enforcement. It takes time for them to follow protocol and go through all the proper channels to get done what you're describing. How long does it take for a satellite like that to orbit into position?"

"Without my calculations nearby, roughly ninety-minutes."

Mom gaped. "You need to stop that satellite before it launches, not after."

"Stopping it before it launches would be ideal, but no one is going to listen to a computer guy without any proof. That's why I haven't gone public. My only authoritative source is fighting for his life right now." He took a deep breath. "Right now, I'm counting on my processes to work and stall the launch."

Dad studied him. "You're that good." The way his dad said it wasn't a question but a surprised revelation.

James prayed he didn't underestimate his own skills. "If my work holds, it's going to be much easier to get law enforcement to reexamine the satellite without concrete proof. The biggest priority right now is making sure all my loved ones are safe."

Mom's eyes widened and her gaze flitted to

Rachel. James turned to find Aria and Gabriella wearing smug grins. Rachel looked like a deer caught in headlights.

Oh. Great. They thought he was calling Rachel a loved one. And if he corrected that notion, he'd just make the situation more awkward.

"Daddy, are we safe?" Ethan asked.

James dropped to his knees, his throat raw. He'd let himself get worked up and had said too much around his boys. He didn't want to lie, so he did the only thing he could think of. He opened his arms to hug them.

FIFTEEN

Rachel tossed and turned in the small twin-size bed. It would be her turn to be on lookout within the hour, and so far sleep had evaded her. This time the room décor wasn't the problem. In fact, the room was painted in a soothing sky blue with wooden blinds.

She'd listened to the crashing of the waves for two hours. Every time she closed her eyes she saw the men with guns. And then Caleb and Ethan in her arms, looking up at her with those adorable smiles, which morphed into James's blue eyes staring right into hers. Her heart pounded so hard she sat up.

She'd told herself she could never love a man with an injured heart, but after seeing him with his family she knew he loved them fiercely. The argument no longer held any weight. And the motherhood thing—she felt her resolve slipping, mainly because she was starting to question if her conviction was based on wisdom or fear.

If she became a mom, even a stepmom, wouldn't she have to face her own childhood again to make sure she didn't repeat the same mistakes her parents had made? If she'd understood Beverly right, she seemed to insinuate that everyone dealt with that no matter their past. It was hard to believe.

Forgiveness wasn't holding her back. She'd truly forgiven her parents. At least, she thought she had. Meredith had made Rachel visit her parents in prison once she'd graduated from beauty school and business school.

Neither her mom nor her dad even mentioned her achievements, nor had they expressed any remorse in their own deeds. They blamed the system, her uncle, fellow dealers…anyone but themselves. Instead they asked her to check on a few "business" items. That's when she knew she had to leave, somewhere far away where none of her relatives could try to pull her back into that life.

"It will still hurt," Meredith had told her after she'd relayed the visit, "but every time it hurts, you take it to God. You take the hurt to Him and then choose to forgive."

She'd lost track of how many nights she'd stared at the ceiling as she was doing right now and whispered, "I choose to forgive." Meredith was right. The pain had almost completely dissipated. Especially the last couple of days. Why was that? Was it seeing the twins surrounded by so much love? Seeing the way the McGuire brothers interacted as a family?

The last thing she wanted was to question her conviction because she was starting to fall for James McGuire. Which brought her back to her original question. Was her conviction to never be a mom based on wisdom or fear? Or was she about to play the justification game? If only Meredith was still alive for her to ask. She knew what Meredith would say, though. *Take it to God.*

She closed her eyes again and prayed.

Her arm shook gently. "Rachel?"

She jerked and almost slammed her forehead into James. She must have dozed off while praying. "What time is it?" she asked, looking around. "Did I miss my shift?"

"No. It's early," he whispered. "Not even five in the morning. Something's happened. Mom disregarded my concerns and made a phone call last night while Dad was on duty. She used a gas station down the road and called the FBI."

That woke her up. Her head pounded. "But you told her not to."

"Both David and Luke found themselves in dangerous situations. Each time, at the last minute, Mom helped by calling in favors. I think she thought she was doing the right thing."

Dread settled in her gut. "Why are you telling me this?"

"I saw a black sedan driving through the neighborhood. They were heading in the direction of the gas station. Dad admitted what she'd done." A ragged sigh escaped his lips. "At least she didn't call from the house."

"It could just be a black sedan."

"If she called at midnight, it'd fit the timeline of the drive time. I can't take the chance that it's not them. I need to get everyone out of here before it's too late. Get ready and meet me in the kitchen as fast as you can."

She'd slept in a pair of sweats Gabriella had loaned her, so she ran to the bathroom, splashed some water in her face, brushed her teeth, pulled her hair back into a loose braid and grabbed her shoes. Her hands shook at the thought of facing the men with guns again.

Everyone but the twins sat at the kitchen table in loungewear and messed-up hair.

James surveyed the group. "So it's possible the crooked NSA agents I told you about have tracked us down. Mom, Dad told me you made a call. I need to know every detail. Don't leave anything out."

Mom stared up at him, her face ashen. "You

have an appointment today at noon at the FBI office in Santa Maria. I made sure to use a public phone, and I never mentioned you by name."

"But you had to mention your name, right, Mom?"

Her shoulders sank as she nodded. "I'm sorry, James, but I knew I would have to pull a lot of strings to get someone to open up the offices on a Sunday. Most of my contacts have all retired. But I found someone who promised they would listen to you."

"Where exactly did you make the call, Mom?"

"There was a pay phone in front of the gas station near the dunes. I'm sorry, James. I really am."

James pulled his hands into fists and exhaled. "You were doing what you thought was best, as am I." James turned to David and Luke. "I need one of you to grab the boys and go."

Gabriella jumped out of her chair. "I'll wake the boys and get them dressed."

Aria joined her.

David exhaled. "I need to stay around here for a while longer, bro, or my chances at getting the conference center acquisition go through the window."

"Your life isn't worth the risk," James said.

"Agreed, but how do you know it's actually at risk?"

He asked his mom to repeat everything she'd said on the phone. After she relayed it, his dad, Luke, David and James argued over the options until they formed a plan. Luke would take Gabriella, Aria and the boys somewhere far away to hide.

"Don't even tell me where," James said. "I don't want to know until this is all over. Just keep them safe."

His parents and David would take the other truck and drive out of town, somewhere north, and hang out there until early afternoon. As long as there weren't any signs of trouble, David would still go to his appointment while his parents packed up and shut down the beach house properly.

"I want you to go with them," James said to Rachel. "When this is all over, I'll come back for you and get you back home."

Her eyes widened. "No. I'm going with you to that FBI appointment. You said you'd have a hard time convincing them." She pointed to her shoulder. "Well, I can help. Hard to ignore a gunshot wound. Besides, I'm an eyewitness to the kidnapping attempts. Last I heard, kidnapping's still in the FBI's jurisdiction, and maybe, by association, that would justify investigating Launch Operations. I can help you get these guys."

James shook his head. "No. I'm leaving in two minutes and heading toward that gas station to keep an eye on the men while they get ready to leave. If they so much as head this way, I'm going to distract them."

"Two heads are better than one," she retorted. "Besides, I have a weapon."

"Which is another reason you should go with my parents," James added.

"I'm carrying," David said.

James's eyes bulged. "Since when?"

"Since I faced the Russian mafia. Pretty sure Luke and Gabriella both have concealed carry permits after their bout with the Mirabella family."

Rachel grabbed her purse and slung it diagonally across her torso. "What are we waiting for?"

James had never been so frustrated at his family and the situation. Ultimately he only had himself to blame. Luke stood guard at the living room window, watching the street. All the lights in the house stayed off except for the light underneath the oven hood in the kitchen.

The boys came out, sleepy but smiling. James leaned down and hugged them. "You're

going to go on a fun trip with Uncle Luke and
your aunts. Okay? And Daddy will try to join
you real soon."

Caleb turned to Rachel. "Are you coming?"

Rachel leaned forward. "Not this time. Hopefully I'll see you soon back at our own houses."
Her eyes shone. "Can I have a hug to hold me
over?"

Caleb and Ethan didn't hesitate. They ran
into her arms. As her head bent down to embrace them, James found it hard to breathe.

She straightened. "We need to go."

Before he could argue with her, she darted
out the back door onto the deck. He looked
over his shoulder to find a sympathetic David
patting his back. "Seems like we attract strong
women. Go keep each other safe." He squeezed
James's shoulder. "I'm counting on hearing
from you once you arrive at the FBI appointment."

James nodded and followed Rachel. The least
he could do was make sure his family could
get away without any trouble. She waited for
him by the white van with one hand inside her
purse, presumably on her gun.

He left the lights off and drove down the
street toward the gas station.

"What's the plan?"

He blew out a breath. "I have no idea."

She pointed to a black sedan parked in the shadows, a block ahead near the gas station. "There it is," she whispered. "James, do you see them anywhere?"

"Not yet."

She pulled out her scissors from her purse. Her eyes glistened in the moonlight. "Think you can use these to puncture the tires?"

He stared at them. They were the same ones so expensive she hesitated to let anyone use them. "Won't it ruin them?"

She shrugged. "I'd say it's worth it to keep them from shooting anyone else."

He reached for the pair, but his hand froze over hers. Her soft skin sent warmth shooting up his arm. Once again she was willing to sacrifice for him, for his family. His brow furrowed at a thought. "If I do this, they'll know for sure we're here."

She looked down at his hand. He couldn't be sure in the darkness but it almost seemed like she blushed.

"The way I see it they already know we're in the area. This just takes away their ability to follow us."

He nodded. The reasoning was sound. "Okay. Wait here."

She followed him out of the vehicle. "You're

supposed to be the analytical one. It's smarter to have a lookout."

He let out a soft growl. He just wanted to keep her safe. They squatted down at the back of the car. He gripped the middle of the shears. "Are we sure this is their car?" he asked.

Her eyes widened. "I'd say so. They're coming this way. Hurry. You've only got about thirty seconds before they spot us."

"I thought I'd have more time. Stay back." The math calculations of the tire pressure and the best place to puncture the tires ran through his head. He turned away from the tire and slammed his fist backward until he felt the blade make contact. A hiss rewarded his effort. He scurried to the front tire and repeated the step.

"Hey!" One of the men sprinted toward the car. The other man pulled out his gun.

"Time's up," Rachel said.

That was an understatement. He grabbed the wrist of her uninjured arm and pulled her into the shadows in between two darkened tourist gift shops.

"Don't hit him. Aim for her," the man yelled at the shooter.

A gunshot rang out. James pulled her wrist so she would duck as he did, but they kept running for the beach. "Did you get hit?"

"No. Don't think they could see us in the shadows." She panted and pulled her wrist out of his hand as she grabbed the stair handles. "Are you sure we should head for the beach?"

"Yes. Counting on using the sea stacks."

"What?" She yelled as she kept running.

"Intertidal—big ocean rocks!" James pulled his weapon out but didn't slow his pace. He pointed the gun straight in the air and pulled the trigger.

Rachel leaped for the sand and ran sideways, her crazed eyes meeting his. "What was that for?"

"To make them hesitate for a second. Think we're shooting back at them." He shoved the gun back in his waistband and ran alongside her. They barely made it to the shadows of the giant dunes in the distance before he heard the thudding of loafers hitting the wooden beach stairs.

The crash of the waves sounded so much more powerful down at this level. The wind blew the small wisps of hair hanging around Rachel's face. The full moon shone bright, peeking through the clouds. It reflected off the deep waters of the ocean. The sand dunes did good work keeping them in shadows, though. They ran shoulder to shoulder. He sucked in the salty air. Running on the loose, coarse sand was harder than he imagined.

"See the rocks ahead? We just need to get behind them. If we run closer to the water, the sand will be firmer." He grabbed her arm and led her. James pulled her in between an out-cropping of rocks, half on the shore, half in the water.

The sounds of crashing waves and wind made it harder to hear what was happening, but it also meant that there was no way the men could hear them. "What are we doing?" she asked, her mouth close to his ear.

He tilted his face toward hers. "Hiding. But I can see them while they can't see us, and if I need to shoot, I will. We have the advantage under this covering."

His blood ran hot remembering what the man had shouted. He should've never let Rachel come. If he could rely on the men to act honorably, he could surrender himself and make them give their word to leave Rachel alone. But how could he trust men who betrayed their country, who purposefully aimed to shoot a woman?

Rachel shivered, either from shock or fighting against the chill the wind brought in the early morning. It had to be barely fifty degrees, if that. His hand drifted, on instinct, and held her hand.

A loud splash sounded in the ocean. Rachel flinched and bumped into James.

"It's seals," he whispered into her ear. "They hang out on that outcropping behind us. They're diving for their breakfast, I think."

She looked up at James. The moonlight only enhanced her beauty. "Wh-when is sunrise?"

"In about an hour. I have no intention of staying here that long." James peeked in the crevice. The men had reached the shoreline. The way they looked both ways confirmed they hadn't seen where James and Rachel had gone.

Now what? He hadn't fully thought out a plan. He reached for Rachel and pulled her closer to one of the larger monolith rocks. He couldn't rest against the rock, however, as it had plenty of jagged edges and was mostly covered in sharp mussel shells. He put a finger at his lips and looked out between the rocks.

The men were yelling at each other, but he couldn't pick up anything but the vibrations of voices. The best-case scenario would be to wait until they moved down the beach then sneak back up to the van.

The ocean waves crashed against their feet again. At least he'd given his family plenty of time to get away. He moved his lips close to

Rachel's head. "As soon as they're out of range, we need to get into the shadows and circle back to the stairs."

She rose on her tiptoes and spoke into his hair. "I'm not sure the incoming tide will let us wait that long."

The water crashed against their feet again, soaking through his shoes. James cringed. She had a point. Rachel looked at him with questioning eyes, but they had no choice. He was no sharpshooter.

He squeezed Rachel's hand. He peeked around the corner again but no longer saw the men. The clouds moved and fully covered the moon. Now all he could see were dark shapes and the whites of her eyes. He strained his ears. Through the crevice, he couldn't make out anything but the small hanging light in the distance, at the top of the long line of beach stairs.

It seemed like now or never. They needed to move before the clouds did. He squeezed her hand. "Go."

Sprinting on wet sand was easy but the moment it transitioned into the loose sand their speed slowed. A gust of wind brushed against his cheeks. Moonlight flickered on the grains of sand. A gunshot rang out. James looked side to side. The men had split up and gone in different directions. They were surrounded.

Rachel fell in front of him. He narrowly avoided stepping on her. She struggled to pop up, but James put his hand underneath her knees and swooped her into his arms.

"What are you doing?" Her arms grasped behind his neck.

He took off running again. His legs burned as he sprinted toward the long line of stairs. "Are you okay? Are you shot?"

"I just tripped when I saw them on either side. James, put me down." She patted his chest. "You're going to hurt yourself."

"There you go, always thinking about my safety, or the boys' safety. How about you just let me take care of you for once?" He huffed as he vaulted up the stairs. "It occurred to me they don't want to risk shooting me. So enjoy the ride."

Sure enough the gunfire ceased.

"I…"

He didn't bother looking at her face. It would distract him from his goal. "How about you make it easier on yourself and me by relaxing?"

She sighed as she leaned her head against his chest. It helped his center of gravity, and James was able to push off the ground harder and faster. Within a minute he reached the van and put her down. "They're right behind us. Buckle up."

SIXTEEN

Rachel's shoulder throbbed like never before. James sped off as a bullet dinged somewhere on the van. Her breathing shuddered as he turned the corner.

"And now we get out of town," he said.

"I've been thinking. There were two vehicles following us earlier. What if there are—"

He jerked the wheel and spun them onto another side street, heading back in the direction of the beach house. "I can't believe I didn't think of that." His knuckles turned white around the steering wheel. He shook his head. "Each time I think we're closer to safety—" He smacked the side of the dash. "I've put everyone I care about in danger."

Rachel remained silent as he sped down the winding street. The way he'd picked her up and carried her because he realized they wouldn't shoot him... Her face warmed at the memory. He slowed at the beach house.

She leaned forward. "The trucks are gone."

James pressed on the brakes and hung his head. His breathing was ragged, and she fought tears of relief back as she knew he must be. She reached for his hand. "They're safe," she whispered.

He squeezed her hand, inhaled sharply and looked back at the road. "But we aren't, not yet. Let's get out of here."

He drove for three hours straight, essentially in circles. They went to every coastal town but Arroyo Grande, as James didn't want to lead anyone near David and his parents. Rachel's ankle swelled slightly. Since James had never given her a chance to run after she'd tripped, she hadn't realize she'd twisted it. She reached down and rubbed it while James filled up with gas, but he didn't want them to go inside the station. Security cameras were likely.

After another hour of tense driving, her stomach growled loudly. James pulled over in front of a small coffee shop in Morro Bay. "We'll grab some food to go, but we don't stay for longer than ten minutes."

Rachel limped slightly to the restrooms. Her ankle wasn't bad, but it wasn't normal, either. In the mirror she tried to calm her hair, which looked as frazzled as she felt. Only a few more hours of driving until they would be safe inside the FBI building. She couldn't wait until then. Would life ever go back to normal? Could she ever see James again as just a neighbor?

She stepped out of the restroom to find James waiting. In one hand he held a carrying tote of lattes while in the other hand he held a plastic bag full of items. He watched out the shop's windows before being satisfied they could go back to the van.

A minivan without mini-people felt wrong. She missed Caleb and Ethan's laugh, something that surprised her. As soon as she opened up her mind to the possibility of being a mother, she suddenly couldn't wait to see them again. She didn't know what to make of it, but she certainly wouldn't voice it aloud.

Once seated, he opened the shopping bag to reveal giant sunglasses and a beach hat for her. "Thought it wouldn't hurt to add a little disguise. Plus, you look good in everything."

She laughed and her cheeks heated. "Believe it or not, I always imagined myself in something like this if I ever went on vacation." Rachel pulled on the floppy hat. She watched the tourists walking along the sidewalks and released a sigh. "If we get out of this, I'm going to start taking vacations on my own, with or without my friends."

"Why haven't you before?"

"I do so much alone. I guess it felt weird to take a vacation alone. And I think deep down it scared me. I'm sure it sounds stupid."

"I get that. I haven't taken the boys on a vacation ever since Nikki passed away."

She frowned. "Because it was too hard?"

"That, and like you, I've thrown myself into work, service and routines. I'm not sure what it'd be like to just rest and have time to think. I didn't realize I was scared of that. Coming here—being forced to stop and hide—has made me face that fear, made me realize it really is time to start embracing life again."

They came from opposite places yet he'd voiced her fears exactly.

He handed her a latte, a cheese Danish and a plastic bag full of ice. "For your ankle."

Her throat constricted at the gesture. He must have noticed her limp. Her eyes stung with tears. "What if you *are* the guy?" The question fell from her lips before she could stop it.

His breath caught. He looked at Rachel and wanted to pull her close, wanted to kiss her. But his arms seemed paralyzed. He wanted to say yes, he was the guy. But he couldn't answer that for her. She needed to be certain before he could open his heart again. He had the boys to think of…

But the way she looked at him melted his heart. He reached for her hands. "Then I'll be patient until you figure that out," he said.

She let go of his hands and moved the bag of ice to her ankle. "Thank you for this." Her voice shook slightly.

"We need to get back on the road." He raked a hand through his hair. Had he messed everything up? That was completely the wrong thing to say, wasn't it? His heart wanted to jump out of his chest. If he stopped and ruminated over his feelings, he wouldn't be able to think straight to get them out of danger. He needed to focus on staying hidden.

She turned on the radio and sipped her coffee in silence as they spent the next few hours methodically going to every town surrounding Santa Maria, until the clock mercifully told him it was time.

"I never thought I'd be so happy to go to an office building," Rachel said.

"I know. I'll probably stand the entire meeting." He exhaled. "I've been sorting out what to say to the agents and the most efficient way to say it." He tapped his fingers on the steering wheel. "And, I know you and I have more to talk about. As soon as we get through this—"

"It's okay, I know what that means. If we need to 'talk,' then you've decided we should just stay neighbors. Let's just let it go, James. Forget I said anything." Her voice sounded tight, clipped.

His jaw tightened. That's what he feared. She wasn't serious about him. "Well, if you ever decide you can't let it go, let me know."

"James—"

He turned to look at her, but her eyes were on the side mirror.

His gut dropped. It wasn't a black vehicle at all, but the dark blue SUV was coming up fast, way past the speed limit. They were only five minutes from the FBI building. He just needed to get them there and they'd be safe. He proceeded to take three left turns to see if they were still following them. "Hold on."

He took a sudden turn. A moment later the SUV joined them. His arms tensed, and he pushed the old van as far as he could. The tires squealed as he took a second turn. The SUV kept its pace. He didn't need another turn to confirm they were after them. "New plan. We drive to the FBI building and drive through the gates if we have to."

Another SUV pulled onto the street ahead of them, blocking their path. James slammed on the brakes. Rachel screamed. They screeched to a halt, coffee sloshing onto the dashboard.

His ears roared. They had known. They had

known he would be heading for the FBI building at noon. How could he have missed that? If they had tracked them down in Pismo Beach because of his mom's phone call at the gas station then they would've heard the appointment being scheduled.

Surrounded by empty office buildings on a Sunday, they had no options for exits. He slammed his palm into the steering wheel. He'd been so careful only to lead them right into a trap.

The phone in the cup holder rang. He stared at it as it rang again. How would they get his number, though? It rang a third time, and he pressed the speaker button.

"Play nice or that red dot on the back of your girlfriend's head is going to get a lot redder."

Rachel didn't recognize the cold, calculating voice, but as James leaned back and looked at the back of her head, he paled. She inhaled sharply.

"Take it easy." James turned to face the window. "What do you want?"

In the passenger-side mirror she could see the red line coming from the SUV behind her. Someone was using a red laser scope on her.

"I think it's very clear what I want, but in case you're not so sure you want to give it to me, I have a call I'd like to patch you through to." The line filled with more static. "Put her on," the man said.

"James?"

James gasped. "Mom?"

"If your father had been alive these past few years, he would've been devastated, James. He'd have wanted you to follow his footsteps, like your brother...be handy."

"That's enough," the man said. The static part of the line ended.

James frowned, his gaze meeting Rachel's.

That was odd. What did his mom mean about his dad being dead?

"You have two motivations now, Mr. McGuire. Get to the launch site and fix what you've done or your mother dies. And, in case you want to make any stops along the way, I've arranged some company to escort you. A wrong turn and you can say goodbye to your girlfriend. Follow the black SUV."

The line went dead. The black vehicle in front of them turned onto the main road. The red dot on the back of her head bounced all around the car until it resettled on her head, filtering through her hair onto her hands. The shooter was definitely in the vehicle behind her.

James looked as if he was going to be sick, but he followed the vehicle ahead. "I'm sorry."

His voice came in a whisper. He glanced at her, pain rimming his eyes. "I'm so sorry."

"How'd they find us?"

James shook his head. "Because I wasn't thinking clearly. If they found us in Pismo then…"

"They knew about the appointment with the FBI." Her voice sounded as dejected as she felt after putting the pieces together. "And they got your phone number from your mom."

She closed her eyes. She'd rather not see the red dot in the vehicle. She couldn't think about what it could do to her or the tears would win. She cleared her throat. "Are you adopted?"

"No. I…I don't know what to make of what Mom said. I'm scared they doped her or maybe the fear made her say odd things."

Rachel exhaled. Beverly had sounded too alert to have been drugged. She was trying to send them a message. Rachel was sure of it.

She replayed the words in her mind. His father wasn't deceased. Follow his footsteps… his brother's…be handy. Rachel's eyes flashed open. She glanced at the phone in the cup holder to make sure it was actually turned off. "I think your dad and brother aren't there with her. 'Be handy'? Maybe they're at a hardware store? Or their meeting?"

James shook his head. "I don't know. None of it made sense."

Rachel kept her head back and riffled in her purse for the phone. She'd never used her burner phone, so it should be clean. And, thanks to his need to think ahead, James had put all his family's numbers in the prepaid phone's contacts. It hurt her eyes and head to scroll down without fully looking at the phone, but she didn't want to alert the men in the vehicles that she was doing anything but cooperating.

She texted Tim and David.

Bev kidnapped. Don't know where. Gunmen taking us 2 launch.

She closed her eyes as she waited for it to send.

The phone vibrated a moment later.

Understood.

What did that mean? Had the men holding Beverly seen the message and texted that? And, if it was from his dad or David, she wanted to ask more. What did they plan on doing with that information?

James seemed oblivious to what she'd just done. His face had lost all color as he followed the black sedan. She grabbed his phone from the cup holder. She didn't have Cynthia's number, but she knew James had called her once from his burner phone. "Don't make any sudden moves. I'm getting your phone and texting Cynthia."

James flinched, clearly fighting not to look at what she was doing. "I don't see how she could help," he said out of the side of his mouth.

"The more people who know, the better chance we have." It hurt her eyes to look down that sharply without moving. She kept the phone low, on her left side. Texting with her left hand proved more difficult, but she managed to text Cynthia.

Taken. Forced to go to launch.

At the least, Cynthia would know why they would no longer be calling. At the best, even though Cynthia didn't know what was going on, maybe she could trust someone with that information and they would look into it. She sighed. Probably not likely.

She grunted. "So much for stretching our legs. How long?"

"We're roughly half an hour away from the launch site."

"Didn't you say it was at an air force base?

Won't there be lots of security?" If the red dot was still on her, someone would notice. That, or the entire facility would need to be crooked.

"There is a main gate, but cleared permanent personnel or contractors can be vouched for. I used to be a cleared contractor, but they removed my remote access. I guess we'll see if someone waves us in or not."

"Can't we tell them the guys in cars are gunmen?" Desperation clawed her way up to her throat, tightening and raising her voice.

"They have my mom," James said. She knew the monotone meant he had resigned himself to the path before him. "If I'm remembering right, there's one curve right before the turn-off. If I can get far enough ahead of the SUV behind us, you could jump out into the trees and run…"

"I'm not taking that chance. Even if I made it with a twisted ankle, they still have your mom…and you." The red dot bounced around and reflected off the glass onto her heart for a brief second. Her heart… What was it James had said about his heart?

My heart broke when I lost Nikki. I don't know if it'll ever be whole again so I don't want to risk further damage by someone who has any doubts.

She took a sudden intake of breath, suddenly

sure of what James had meant about waiting to talk until she couldn't let it go. "James?"

"Yes?" His voice was soft but strained.

"I can't let it go," she said. She sucked in a shaky breath. She'd never, ever, told a man she loved him. Never before had she let herself feel so much affection for one person. "I can't let you go."

His eyes met hers. His mouth sloped into a half smile. His grip tightened around the steering wheel. "So how about we figure out how to survive this?"

She stretched her left hand toward him without shifting in her seat. He grabbed it and squeezed. The truth was, even if he did everything these men wanted him to do, it didn't seem likely they would let them go. Her breathing turned hot as the truth hit her. She needed to be prepared for the worst.

James followed the sedan off of Highway 1 and the air force gate came into view. The buildings were adorned with terra-cotta roofs and surrounded by palm trees. In the center of the beautifully decorated landscape a rocket monument stood with the NASA logo. The side of a rocket and a sliver of the ocean could be seen between the distant hills.

It seemed a shame to come to such a beautiful place only to die.

SEVENTEEN

James approached the gate. The red dot on Rachel's shirt disappeared, and she released a shaky laugh. He never let go of her hand.

The black vehicle in front of him was waved through the gate at record speed, confirming his suspicion that someone in there was a crooked government man. An armed guard walked around the van, peeking in windows. The man at the gate waved them through. The moment the minivan passed the barricade, the navy SUV behind them turned around and drove away without entering.

Rachel breathed a sigh of relief. Unfortunately, James knew they weren't out of danger yet. And his mom…he sucked in a breath. Were they hurting her?

They passed the buildings until they were on a road leading into the hills. "I've only been here once," he mentioned, trying to remember how long it would take to get to the site. "Just past those hills is the launch site."

"Don't you have to go to every takeoff?"

"Yes, but I'm stationed at Mission Control, closer to home. This is the Launch Control Center. They hand it off to us the moment the booster clears the tower." His nerves were rebelling against his calm, cool exterior. His stomach fluttered and his left knee jiggled, trying to help the excess anxiety escape.

His blood ran hot through his veins. He was falling hard for this beautiful, kind, brave woman sitting next to him, and he wasn't sure he'd live to tell her. He had wanted to reciprocate when she had said she couldn't let him go, but he had faltered, his throat choking on the emotion.

They followed the sedan around a bend and pulled to a stop. The two men from the black vehicle opened their doors. Each one held a gun. The driver looked familiar, from the church, but the other one was different.

"Get out," one man hollered.

James opened the door and stood, only to have the man shove him hard against the car. His elbow connected with the edge of the door frame, searing pain shooting into his shoulder. "That's for not coming quietly the first time."

Judging by the red welt on the man's wrist, he was referring to the church. "He still needs to be able to type," the other muttered. "She had a gun in her purse."

The man in front of James patted him down. He straightened. "Don't have my gun, huh?" He pulled his fist back.

James stiffened his stomach muscles a second before the fist made impact. All the air rushed from his lungs as he buckled.

"We've got eyes on us," the other gunman said. "The boss is waiting."

James straightened, sucking in a breath of air. Thankfully his martial arts training had helped him take the punch without injury. It didn't make it painless, though. The man pushed him forward to walk toward the control center.

Rachel limped in front of the car and they were side by side again. Her wide eyes searched his face for signs he was all right. They bumped shoulders and walked forward on the path.

Up the metal stairs, they found themselves in a pristine-white hallway. They passed two elevators that, if memory served right, would've taken them to launch viewing.

"Two doors down to the right," the gunman uttered. James peeked a look back and realized they'd holstered their guns. The cameras in the hallway may have been responsible for that. So maybe there were members of security that weren't a part of this?

He opened the door and stepped inside first only to see his supervisor, Brian Holland, standing in the room without windows. A small table sat in the middle with one lone laptop and a folding chair. The new gunman stayed outside of the door while the bulky one stood guard on the inside of the door.

"Brian, what's going on? Why would you be behind something like this?"

"I could ask you the same question, James. You could have had a lucrative bonus and promotion if you had come to me instead of pulling this stunt." He waved at the computer.

"What good would money do me if it launches? The country will be shoved into the 1800s."

The bulky guard shuffled uneasily.

Brian shrugged. "Not my problem. I'll be long gone in a country far, far away."

James looked right at the guard. "So, are you the NSA mole? Are you going to be long gone, too? Leave your family here to suffer your actions? What about Derrick? Was that your doing?"

The man jerked forward, but Brian held his hand up. "You're just like your wife. Sticking your nose where it doesn't belong."

The gravity of his words washed over him. James launched forward. His fist hit Brian squarely in the jaw before he could even process.

Rachel cried out. James spun, his arms up. The guard had her arm twisted behind her back. Her chin up, he could see the pain in her eyes. Her purse dangled from its diagonal hold.

"Let her go!"

"I think you've forgotten what can happen to women you care for," Brian seethed, his hand rubbing his red jaw. He waved a hand at the man, who released Rachel. She rubbed her elbow and took a giant step away from the man.

James took ragged breaths. His eyes blurred. "Why? Why'd you kill Nikki?"

"Same reason you're here. She threatened to meddle with a very lucrative spy satellite. I told her if she told anyone her family would die. I offered her a promotion. She started taking sick days, and I couldn't trust she'd stay quiet."

"Why not kill me, too?"

"Oh, I thought about it, but it'd be a little more suspicious if both of you passed away so soon. We watched you. It seemed your wife kept her word about staying quiet. You didn't seem to pose a threat, and you were a valuable member of the team. Now I wished I'd killed you when I had a chance." He grinned. "But thanks to your wife, we knew it was time to have a helpful NSA agent assigned to us." He waved at the gunman.

"What have they got on you?" James asked. "Must be big to sell your soul."

"Shut up," the agent spat.

James looked up at the ceiling. His boss, his wife's murderer, was standing in front of him, and he could do nothing.

Brian pointed at the desk. "You have an hour to repair what you've done, or the women start feeling the consequences." He walked to the door. "The moment he's done, get hold of me."

Rachel's eyes met James's. She nodded, her eyes soft.

James sighed and sat down on the metal folding chair. He typed his remote access into the laptop, and this time it worked. An hour was going to be cutting it close to undo all his work. It had been a masterpiece of programming that'd taken him eight hours solid. To destroy it without faulting the rest of the system would be difficult. "I'll be able to work a lot faster if we had water, and I wasn't worried about her comfort."

The gunman scowled. "Just start working." He knocked on the door. It opened slightly and the man stuck his head out. "Water and another chair," he said to the other guard.

It was tempting to rush the man, but the empty room amplified every move he made, especially while sitting on a metal folding chair. And, the man's gun was on the other side of his jacket, farthest from his reach.

Rachel opened her mouth, as if ready to whisper something to James, but the guard was back inside already. James set back to work. His fingers flew through his more native language as he typed the Linux code to retrieve and change his processes until they were rendered ineffective.

Before long the rest of the world disappeared. Out of the blue when he typed "target file," his chest constricted. His wife had been a target. The clock at the top of the screen told him he only had minutes to spare. The hour had passed by too quickly.

He pressed forward, typing the next commands. "Process." Something he didn't have time to do. Then "kill" followed by the parameters and then "kill all" and "execute." He couldn't breathe. He leaned back in the chair, the words a blur in front of him. She'd stayed quiet to protect him. She'd died for him, for them. Unshed tears choked his throat.

"James," Rachel said softly. She leaned forward and placed a hand on his shoulder. "I'm so sorry. It's a lot to take in." She glanced at the screen. "Coding is a violent language."

He coughed. "Yes."

"Get it done," the man shouted.

He set the system to reboot, but hesitated to tell the guard anything. He needed time to think. How could they get out of this situation? How could he make sure that Nikki's sacrifice wasn't in vain? That he would still live to raise their children? How could he save Rachel and his mom?

The computer screen flashed that the changes had been saved and complete.

"Out of time," the man said, approaching.

That was what James was afraid of.

Rachel watched the NSA agent approach.

"Did you finish?" the man grunted.

James nodded mutely.

The man pressed a few buttons on his phone. "Yeah. Test it?" he asked into the phone. He stared down at James. "Good. You can shut down his access." He hung up. "Look's like you did your job. Get up."

"Wait. Release my mom and Rachel now."

"That's not how this works." He gestured for Rachel to go first toward the door. The man stood sideways, watching them both. He reached for the door handle when Rachel's waist vibrated.

He shoved her against the wall so fast she couldn't brace herself for impact. The air rushed out of her lungs. The back of her head slammed against the drywall, bouncing forward. Her chin hit the man's forearm, pressed into her collarbone. She gasped, trying to fill her lungs. His rough hands pulled the phone from inside the thick waistband she'd hidden it.

"'Threat removed,'" he read. He shook the phone in her face with his right hand. "What's this supposed to mean?"

Rachel inhaled again, trying to ignore the pain. "That his mom is safe," she said, her eyes darting to James.

The man turned to follow her gaze as she slammed her knee in between his legs. He jerked backward, but the self-defense move only seemed to make him angrier. Before she could react, James landed a blow to the side of the man's face.

The man stumbled backward, reaching for his holster. Rachel whipped her foot at his hand. The moment it made contact she cried out as it put too much pressure on her injured ankle. Her leg almost gave out.

James jumped him, twisting back the hand

that reached for the gun. Rachel grabbed the weapon from the holster and stumbled back into the door just as it was opening.

"What's going—" The second guard opened the door with his gun raised. Rachel pressed her gun into the back of his neck and shoved him forward. She maneuvered quickly, barely catching the open door with her hip. "Drop it," she said.

James had the other man on the ground as the second guy dropped his gun. Rachel kicked it away with her good foot. "Now lie down on the ground."

James ran for the kicked gun and pointed it at the first guard who was already up on one knee.

"Stay back." He made his way to Rachel. He held the door open with one hand, moving their way backward into the hallway. He grabbed the door handle and shoved it closed at the last second.

He took off down the hallway, making sure she was keeping up with him. "I wasn't going to be a match for that guy, or I would've grabbed their phones. They won't be detained for long." He grabbed her hand and pulled her along faster down the hall. "You were brilliant. How'd you know my mom was safe?"

She pumped her arms, trying to ignore the

throbbing in her ankle. "I didn't want to get your hopes up. I texted your dad and David... and Cynthia."

"I could kiss you." He flashed that half smile that made her want to swoon.

She tried to laugh it off as her neck tingled with the thought. "Too bad we're running for our lives."

"I didn't leave empty-handed." He waved a laminated badge at Rachel with a smirk. "I think this is our ticket out of here."

He slid the badge across a reader next to the stairway door. It beeped and opened. She hobbled after him. Her ankle smarted again, but she wouldn't let it slow her down. "James?" She reached for his arm. "Can you stop the launch?"

He nodded. "I think so, but I want you out of danger."

"We won't go too long running through Launch Control with guns before someone helpful finds us. I don't think they're all crooked."

"Let's hope you're right." He surprised her by taking the stairs two at a time...going up.

"Why up?" She panted, two steps behind him.

"It's where the server room is." He stopped at the next door, his hand on the handle. "Let's stop this launch."

The door below them slammed. One of the

gunmen must have already gotten out. James threw an arm around Rachel's waist and helped her speed down an identical hallway until he got to an unlabeled door. He swiped the badge, it beeped, and they stepped inside. Without a window, she couldn't tell how close the gunmen were to following them.

The hum of the room almost overwhelmed her. Electronics lined the entire room.

James pressed what looked like a flat rack of monitors and a laptop popped out. "How about you get us that attention we want?" He gestured his head toward the ceiling where a black orb hung, a security camera.

She waved her gun at it like a crazy woman. "If that doesn't get someone's attention I don't know what will." She looked over her shoulder. "How can you get in without remote access?"

"This room isn't remote. It's live. I can shut this baby down in real time." The sounds the keyboard made sounded like rapid gunfire. Someone shouted, followed by thumps and thuds in the hallway. Rachel moved to stand in front of James and pointed her gun at the door.

"What do you think you're doing?"

"Guarding you so you can get it done," she said.

"I'm not letting another woman I love die for me." The door flung open. James's left arm swung out in front of her, throwing her backward as he jumped in front to face the gunman in the doorway.

EIGHTEEN

"Stand down," the man yelled.

James blinked. He wasn't either of the men that had been chasing them. "Are you security?"

"NSA," the man answered.

"James," Rachel said, "it's the man who took Cynthia to the hospital."

The man lowered his weapon. "I'm Agent Thorne. You're James and Rachel?"

James exhaled and reached a hand out to Rachel. "You okay?"

She nodded and took his hand to get up.

"Derrick woke from ICU," Thorne explained. "He had a visual on the man who ran him off the road. We got your text from Cynthia right after we were able to figure out the mole and find any other compromised agents." Just past his shoulder he saw other agents reading the cuffed gunmen their rights. Next to them stood a gathering group of men in camouflage, likely air force security.

"Derrick wants to know if you can shut down the launch."

James exhaled. "Give me two more minutes." He turned to the keyboard and continued to type, overriding commands until "Launch Failure" appeared on the screen. He stepped away, shoulders sagging in relief.

Rachel placed a hand on his shoulder. "You did it," she whispered.

"I'm sorry to do this, but I need to ask you both questions separately while we secure the rest of the building," Agent Thorne said.

"And I'll be glad to…after I see Brian Holland in cuffs." James stood his ground.

Thorne put his hands on his waist, mulling it over. "I think I can help with you that."

James reached for Rachel.

"I'm afraid she needs to stay here," Thorne interjected.

Rachel smiled. "Go ahead, James. I'll be fine."

He followed Thorne and another agent to the elevator.

"We found Holland had wired money to the Caymans," Thorne explained. "We've traced it back to a terrorist group. We also discovered a falsified passport and airline ticket to

France, and an apartment set up in Andorra where there's no extradition treaty."

In other words, they didn't know the whole story. Approaching the top floor, James shared with Thorne what Holland had admitted about ordering a hit on Nikki. "Make sure Derrick knows."

Thorne crossed his arms over his chest, his expression somber. "I understood your wife was once part of the NSA family. You can be assured she'll get justice." Thorne pointed to a window where they could see straight into the launch observation room. "Wait here."

James crossed his arms over his chest and braced himself. He could see Brian's smug face as he sat with the other executives. Agent Thorne took a guard and walked into the room. Thorne pointed at Brian and the guard moved in front of him. As Brian held his hands up and turned around, his eyes met James's. Brian's eyes widened with awareness as he was handcuffed.

James exhaled. For the first time in weeks… no, years, he felt peace.

Thorne returned and escorted James to a room to give his statement. An hour later, when they were finally done, James leaned back in his chair. "Where's Rachel?"

Thorne checked his phone. "We released her.

Last I heard she asked to lie down in the van while she waited for you."

As James made his way back down to the ground floor, he called his mom, dad and David. After assurances they were safe and unharmed, Mom explained what happened on her end. "I'm so glad Rachel contacted your dad. He called that FBI agent I had set an appointment up with. They surrounded the beach house and took out those creeps before I could blink. Now you boys can't get in any more danger because I'm out of favors to call in."

"That's great, Mom, but why were you at the beach house? That wasn't the plan."

"We left town as promised but right ahead of us on the highway were two guys in suits, hightailing it out of town. They were driving a government-issued black sedan. We figured the threat had passed. Believe me, I didn't think there was another set of them or we'd never have returned."

James closed his eyes, unbelievably thankful that everyone was safe.

"I've heard from Luke. The boys are fine," his mom said. She passed on their location. James couldn't wait to see the boys again and finally be able to tell them with certainty that they were safe.

He said his goodbyes and approached the

van. But there was no sign of Rachel. He peeked in the passenger window and found the passenger seat fully reclined. She was fast asleep and more beautiful than ever.

Sleep had been nonexistent for both of them the past few days. And while he finally felt peace, his body still hummed with adrenaline. Rachel deserved to sleep. He just hoped she wouldn't mind one side trip to pick up the boys.

Rachel stretched and yawned and realized she was in a moving car, in the dark. She tried to sit up and strained against a seat belt.

James chuckled. "Sleep well?"

She flicked the lever and sat up. "How long have I been asleep?"

"A few hours. You didn't so much as twitch."

"I don't remember ever being so exhausted in my life." She rubbed her eyes and noted they were on a freeway filled with lights. "Is everything okay?"

He smiled. "Better than okay."

Rachel bit her lip. Had she dreamed he'd said she was a woman he loved? She fidgeted, not sure how to bring it up. "Um, where are we?"

"Ten minutes away from our stop."

He was grinning from ear to ear. She'd never seen him like this, excited and secretive.

"Which is?" she pressed.

"Rachel, you had your receptionist clear your schedule this week, right?"

She felt her eyebrows raise but said nothing.

"I was wondering if you could take a couple days off while I pick up the boys."

Her mouth dropped. "It's going to take that long to reach them?"

"No, it's going to take that long to enjoy some time off with them. I was thinking about how you and I never take vacations. They happen to be somewhere pretty fun. Have you ever been to Disneyland?"

She gasped. She couldn't help it.

James laughed. "I'll get you your own room. I'll even buy you clothes in the Disney Store."

The reality hit her. She didn't want to owe James anything. "I couldn't let you do that," Rachel said.

His face sobered. "I could never repay you for what you've done for the boys, what you've done for me. Please let me do this little thing." He shrugged. "Besides, I was just given a promotion and a raise."

"Oh?"

"Apparently someone needed to take Brian Holland's job immediately. I said only if I got a couple weeks off first."

Rachel laughed. "Oh, well, if you put it that way. Okay."

She couldn't help but stare at his profile. The city lights flashed past his face. Should she bring up what he'd said in the server room? It'd be too awkward if he'd said it accidentally. Rachel sighed. Well, it could wait until after Disneyland...one of the top three places she'd wanted to visit someday.

James parked and hustled her to the gates of Disneyland. Thankfully, her feet had been elevated the entire time on the drive, so her ankle felt significantly better. Still, he held his arm out for support.

"It's so dark. Do you know where the boys are?"

"Yes. Luke and I picked a meeting spot," he answered. "I think we barely made it just in time." He paid for the tickets, and she walked into Disneyland for the first time.

The street lanterns in the courtyard dimmed and music streamed through the speakers lined all around the park. Kids squealed, parents clapped, and most people sat wherever they'd been standing. Rachel and James stood on the back edge of the crowd. "How will we ever find them in this crowd? Why are they all sitting?"

"I'm not worried about that right now. The boys are in safe hands." He grinned. "I think you need to see this."

Shades of blue, purples and pinks illuminated the Sleeping Beauty Castle. Spotlights streamed into the sky, moving around. Shimmering sparkles shot out into the sky simultaneously from all different directions. A glowing Tinker Bell glided through the evening sky. "How'd they do that?"

Sonic booms that would normally terrify her sent shivers of delight and wonder up her spine. Light exploded above the castle in a dazzling array of shapes and colors. She grabbed James's arm instinctively and gaped in awe at the beauty and wonder of it all. "I've seen fireworks before but this…"

In her peripheral she noticed James wasn't paying attention to the show at all. He watched her. The lights in the sky reflected in his eyes. "You're missing it," she said.

He shook his head. "I'm watching the most beautiful thing here."

She eyed him. "You wanted to surprise me with this."

"I had hoped you'd like it."

In that moment she knew she hadn't dreamed his words in the server room. She reached for his hands and stepped closer. Fireworks exploded all around them, as if shimmering diamonds were falling from the sky. "As a kid I dreamed about coming here." She shook her head. "You make it easy to forget all about my past," she said.

"In favor of a good future?" he asked.

She blinked slowly. "Only if it's with you."

He gently moved her hair behind her shoulders and leaned forward. Her cheeks heated as "Kiss the Girl" poured through the speakers.

"May I?" James whispered.

The moment his lips touched hers it was like…well, it was like fireworks.

EPILOGUE

The vibrating was so annoying. Rachel rolled over and opened her eyes. "Who is calling me on Saturday morning?"

In the six months since she'd arrived home from Disneyland, she'd taken to working weekdays only. The first time she'd limited her schedule to forty hours, she'd worried she'd have a panic attack. Instead, James and the boys had kept her busy. Now, forty hours was more than enough for her.

Last weekend, for instance, they rode on a hayride, hiked through a corn maze and painted pumpkins. They'd taught her how to play, how to have fun.

She peeked at the phone.

Where are you?

She couldn't help but smile. James was a

morning person. It simultaneously drove her crazy and amused her. She texted back.

At home, about to get started on my long To Do list.

It vibrated immediately.

You were sleeping in, weren't you?

She cracked up. She knew he'd see right through her.

I wanted to throw a pebble at your window. Will this work instead?

She frowned. Why would he want to throw a pebble? To get her attention? She kicked off her covers and shuffled to the bedroom window. Pulling back the curtains, she looked down.

The red, orange and yellow leaves had been raked in their adjoining yards to spell *Marry Me?*

James stood at the end of the piles wearing a suit, holding a phone.

Rachel put a hand over her mouth. She squealed, darted into the bathroom, brushed her teeth and ran a comb through her hair. It was a good thing that man knew she got ready fast. She launched down the stairs and flung open the front door.

She almost ran into James, on his knee, on her patio. He held an open, black ring box with a sparkling diamond inside. "Rachel Cooper, would you—"

"Yes!" she blurted. She put a hand over her mouth and laughed. She waved at the yard. "Sorry. I thought you'd already asked."

He jumped up, a giant smile spread on his face. "I love you."

"I love you, too." She wrapped her hands around his neck and pulled him close. His hands tightened around her waist as he kissed her.

She looked up at the beautiful display in her yard. "I didn't think we had this many leaves between both yards."

James gestured behind him. Every yard in the entire cul-de-sac was void of leaves. "No one minded letting me rake for them."

Two giant leaf piles closer to the oak tree shifted. The boys burst up through them. "Surprise!"

James laughed, but didn't release his hold on her, and she hoped he never did. "Good job, guys."

"She gonna marry us, huh, Dad," Ethan said. Both boys were nodding, and even though it didn't sound like a question, they were waiting for an answer.

Rachel released her arms from James and waved them close. They ran for her and barreled into her waiting arms. James helped lift them up until they were all huddled in a group hug.

The boys kissed her cheeks and she laughed, staring right into her future husband's loving eyes.

"You were right," she said. "God does set the lonely in families."

* * * * *

Dear Reader,

It was early spring with unseasonably warm temperatures. I opened the windows for some fresh air but left the blinds down as I cleaned the house. Usually I put in earphones and crank up the tunes as I clean. It only took an hour to forget that the construction crew across the street could hear everything, including my singing. The embarrassment was enough to make me wonder how much neighbors know about each other just from close proximity. This sparked the idea of James and Rachel.

I love writing about the McGuire brothers. I particularly enjoyed writing James. My own hunky hero, also known as my husband, works in an information technology department and helped me with the terminology. A congressional report written on the threat of an electromagnetic weapon and a desperate need for a haircut provided the rest of the ideas.

I love to hear from readers. Feel free to contact me through my website, writingheather. com.

Blessings,
Heather Woodhaven

REQUEST YOUR FREE BOOKS!
2 FREE WHOLESOME ROMANCE NOVELS IN LARGER PRINT
PLUS 2 FREE MYSTERY GIFTS

✻✻✻✻✻✻✻✻✻✻✻✻✻✻✻✻✻✻✻✻✻✻✻✻

HEARTWARMING™

✻✻✻✻✻✻✻✻✻✻✻✻✻✻✻✻✻✻✻✻✻✻✻✻

Wholesome, tender romances

WESTERN (WP) PROMISES

YES! Please send me **The Western Promises Collection** in Larger Print. This collection begins with 3 FREE books and 2 FREE gifts (gifts valued at approx. $14.00 retail) in the first shipment, along with the other first 4 books from the collection! If I do not cancel, I will receive 8 monthly shipments until I have the entire 51-book Western Promises collection. I will receive 2 or 3 FREE books in each shipment and I will pay just $4.99 US/ $5.89 CDN for each of the other four books in each shipment, plus $2.99 for shipping and handling per shipment. *If I decide to keep the entire collection, I'll have paid for only 32 books, because 19 books are FREE! I understand that accepting the 3 free books and gifts places me under no obligation to buy anything. I can always return a shipment and cancel at any time. My free books and gifts are mine to keep no matter what I decide.

272 HCN 3070 472 HCN 3070

Name	(PLEASE PRINT)	
Address		Apt. #
City	State/Prov.	Zip/Postal Code

Signature (if under 18, a parent or guardian must sign)

Mail to the **Reader Service**:

IN U.S.A.: P.O. Box 1867, Buffalo, NY 14240-1867
IN CANADA: P.O. Box 609, Fort Erie, Ontario L2A 5X3

WPBPA16R